P9-CFO-587

"I Wanted To Be Alone With You."

"We could have been alone walking down the pier."

"That did occur to me, but you're not dressed for the cold night." He lowered his gaze as if pondering the pattern his fingers were painting on her palm. He raised his eyes a moment later and she gasped. Gentleness and humor were gone, that grim god of the desert back. She shuddered with the fierceness of her response. "You know where I really want to be alone with you. In my place. In my bed."

Dear Reader,

When I wrote "The End" in my first Silhouette Desire trilogy, Throne of Judar, I was already dreaming of a sequel in the neighboring allied kingdom of Zohayd. I am so excited to be realizing that dream and beginning my new trilogy, Pride of Zohayd, starring princes Shaheen, Harres and Amjad.

The trilogy kicks off with the youngest brother, Shaheen, who is about to sacrifice his freedom for his kingdom in a marriage of state. Then he meets the woman of his dreams and everything changes. But like every profound love story, everything is against them, from his commitments to a brewing conspiracy that could topple the royal house of Zohayd and plunge the whole region into chaos. The worst part is that his beloved Johara and her father are the main suspects or at least seem to be pivotal instruments in his family's plotted downfall.

Will his love stand the test of shocking revelations and discoveries? Will he and his brothers succeed in uncovering the conspiracy and defending their throne and kingdom before it's too late?

I adored writing Shaheen and Johara's story, and I hope you enjoy reading it! I would love to hear from you at oliviagates@gmail.com. You can also visit me on the web at www.oliviagates.com.

Enjoy, and thanks for reading.

Olivia Gates

OLIVIA GATES

TO TAME A SHEIKH

Silhouette®
Desire

Published by Silhouette Books
America's Publisher of Contemporary Romance

If you purchased this book without a cover you should be aware that this book is stolen property. It was reported as "unsold and destroyed" to the publisher, and neither the author nor the publisher has received any payment for this "stripped book."

Recycling programs for this product may not exist in your area.

ISBN-13: 978-0-373-73063-6

TO TAME A SHEIKH

Copyright © 2010 by Olivia Gates

All rights reserved. Except for use in any review, the reproduction or utilization of this work in whole or in part in any form by any electronic, mechanical or other means, now known or hereafter invented, including xerography, photocopying and recording, or in any information storage or retrieval system, is forbidden without the written permission of the editorial office, Silhouette Books, 233 Broadway, New York, NY 10279 U.S.A.

This is a work of fiction. Names, characters, places and incidents are either the product of the author's imagination or are used fictitiously, and any resemblance to actual persons, living or dead, business establishments, events or locales is entirely coincidental.

This edition published by arrangement with Harlequin Books S.A.

For questions and comments about the quality of this book please contact us at Customer_eCare@Harlequin.ca.

® and TM are trademarks of Harlequin Books S.A., used under license. Trademarks indicated with ® are registered in the United States Patent and Trademark Office, the Canadian Trade Marks Office and in other countries.

Visit Silhouette Books at www.eHarlequin.com

Printed in U.S.A.

Books by Olivia Gates

Silhouette Desire

**The Desert Lord's Baby* #1872
**The Desert Lord's Bride* #1884
**The Desert King* #1896
†*The Once and Future Prince* #1942
†*The Prodigal Prince's Seduction* #1948
†*The Illegitimate King* #1954
Billionaire, M.D. #2005
***To Tame a Sheikh* #2050

*Throne of Judar
†The Castaldini Crown
**Pride of Zohayd

OLIVIA GATES

has always pursued creative passions—singing and many handicrafts. She still does, but only one of her passions grew gratifying enough, consuming enough, to become an ongoing career. Writing.

She is most fulfilled when she is creating worlds and conflicts for her characters, then exploring and untangling them bit by bit, sharing her protagonists' every heart-wrenching heartache and hope, their every heart-pounding doubt and trial, until she leads them to an indisputably earned and gloriously satisfying happy ending.

When she's not writing, she is a doctor, a wife to her own alpha male and a mother to one brilliant girl and one demanding Angora cat. Visit Olivia at www.oliviagates.com.

To Mom, my daughter and Maria.
I hope you know how much each of you helped me
in writing this book. Love you all.

One

Johara Nazaryan had come to see the only man she'd ever love.

Before he married someone else.

Her heart sputtered on a mixture of anticipation, dread and despondence as her eyes scanned the throngs of top-fashion, highest-class denizens of the party being thrown in his honor.

There was still no sign of Shaheen Aal Shalaan.

She drew in a choppy breath and pressed deeper into her corner, hoping to continue avoiding attention. She was thankful for the extra time to compose herself even as she cursed it for giving her more of a chance to work herself up.

She still couldn't believe she'd decided to see him after twelve years.

Oh, she'd drunk in every drop of news of him for all those years, had stolen glimpses of him whenever she was near where she'd heard he'd be from the time she'd started traveling on her own. But this time, she was determined to walk up to Shaheen and say, *Long time no see.*

Shaheen. To the world he was a prince of the wealthy desert kingdom of Zohayd, the youngest of King Atef Aal Shalaan's three sons from the deceased queen Salwa. He was also a businessman who'd risen in the past six years to become one of the most respected powers in the worlds of construction and transportation.

To Johara he'd always be the fourteen-year-old boy who'd saved her life twenty years ago.

She was six then, on her first day in Zohayd, where she'd come to live in the royal palace with her family. Her Armenian-American father had been appointed first assistant to the royal jeweler, Nazeeh Salah. It had been "Uncle" Nazeeh, her father's mentor, who'd suggested her name, *jewel* in Arabic.

During her father's interview with the king, she'd slipped onto the terrace and ended up falling off its balustrade and dangling from the ledge. At her screams, everyone had come running. Unable to reach her, her father had thrown her a rope noose to slip around her wrist. As she'd tried to put it on, someone below her had urged her to let go. With panic bursting in her heart, she'd looked down.

And she'd seen him.

He'd seemed too far away to be able to catch her. But as her parents had screamed for her to hang on, she'd let go of the ledge and plummeted down the thirty-foot drop, just knowing he would.

And as fast and precise and powerful as the hawk he was named for, he had. He'd swooped in, plucked her from midair and welcomed her into the haven of his arms.

She still dissected those fraught moments from time to time. She knew she would have been able to slip the rope on. But she'd chosen to trust her safety to that magnificent creature who'd looked up at her with strength and assurance radiating from his fiery-brown eyes.

From that day on, she'd known. She'd always be his. And not only because he'd saved her. With every day that passed, the knowledge that he was the most incredible person she'd ever met had solidified, as he became her older brother Aram's best friend and far more than that to her.

But as she'd grown older, she'd realized that her dream of being his one day was impossible.

Shaheen was a prince. She was the daughter of a servant. Even though her father had become the royal jeweler, who both designed new jewelry for the royal family and had the all-important responsibility of maintaining the nation's highest treasure, the Pride of Zohayd royal jewels, he was still an underling, a foreigner who came from a poor background and had worked his way to his current position through his extraordinary talent.

And then, Shaheen wouldn't have looked at her that way even if she were the daughter of the noblest family in Zohayd. He had always been incredibly nice to her, but when it came to romantic partners, he'd had the world's most beautiful, sophisticated women falling at his feet from the time he turned seventeen. Back then, she'd been certain she possessed no beauty and would never attain any sophistication. But she'd found it enough to be near him, to love him.

For eight blissful years, Shaheen had offered her indulgence and friendship. To stay near him, she'd chosen to remain with her father when her parents had separated when she was twelve and her French mother had left Zohayd to go back home and continue her career in fashion design.

Then, suddenly, it was over. Just before her fourteenth birthday, Shaheen had abruptly pulled away from both her brother and her. Aram had told her that Shaheen thought it time to stop fraternizing with the "help" to observe his role as a prince of Zohayd.

Though she couldn't believe it of Shaheen and thought Aram's bitterness had other origins she couldn't guess at, Shaheen's sudden distance was still a wake-up call.

For, really, what did she have to look forward to but to love him, unrequitedly, until he one day entered the marriage of state that was his destiny? He might even have turned away from her because he suspected her feelings for him and was being cruel to be kind. His withdrawal *had* influenced her decision to leave. A few weeks after her birthday, she'd left Zohayd to live in France with her mother. She'd never returned.

Ever since that day, Johara had found comfort from the sense of loss only when she found news of Shaheen, saw that he was doing phenomenally well on every front. She'd felt she was entitled to hold on to that secret, one-sided love.

But now, the blade was about to fall and she'd never again have the right to indulge her emotions, even in the privacy of her heart and mind. And she had to see him. *Really* see him. One last time...before he committed himself to another.

She'd slipped into the farewell party that one of his business partners, Aidan McCormick, was throwing for him in New York City. If anyone questioned her presence, she'd easily defend her right to be there. As a jewelry and fashion designer who'd been making a splash beyond France in the past couple of years, she was considered one of the glitterati who were expected to stud such a function.

But validating her presence wasn't the difficult part. That was still to come. Working up the nerve to approach Shaheen.

She was praying one thing would happen when she did. That she'd find out that she'd blown him all out of proportion in her mind, and her feelings for him, as well.

Suddenly, a wave of goose bumps swept her from toes to scalp.

She turned around, the rustle of her taffeta dress magnified in her ears.

Shaheen was here.

For a long moment, she couldn't see him. But the people-packed space receded into a void where his presence radiated like a beacon. Not from the entrance, where her gaze had been glued for the past two hours, but from the other side of the room. It made no sense, until she realized he must have used McCormick's private elevator.

His aura, his vibe, hit her like a gut punch.

Then she saw him. Only him.

Everything stilled inside her. In awe. In confusion.

He'd towered over her before, though she'd been five foot seven at fourteen. Now she stood six feet wearing two-inch heels, and he still outstripped her by what appeared to be half a foot. Had she never realized how imposing he was?

No. This wasn't the Shaheen she remembered. This was new.

He'd been twenty-two the last time she'd seen him up close. She'd seen him in the flesh half a dozen times since, most recently a year ago, across a ballroom in Cannes. But during those stolen sightings, she'd barely gotten more than an impression of vitality and virility, of class and power. She'd seen photographs and footage of him throughout the years, but it was clear that neither memory, nor sightings from afar nor photographic evidence had transmitted any measure of the truth.

Sure, he'd been like a god to her anyway, but it seemed there were levels of godhood. And his present rank was at the top of the scale. A desert god, forged from its heat and hardness and harshness, from its mystery and moodiness and magnificence.

His all-black formal silk suit and shirt clung to a breadth that was almost double his younger size. There wasn't an inch of padding to his shoulders, no boosting of the power of his chest, no accentuation to the hardness of his abdomen and thighs or the slimness of his waist and hips. If he'd had the lithe power of a young hawk before, he now packed the powerhouse majesty of a full-grown, seasoned one.

And that was before taking the changes to his face into account. He'd always been what the media had called spectacular, with that wavy mane of deepest tobacco hair, those unique fiery eyes a contrast to his natural tan. Now, with every trace of softness and youth chiseled away to leave a bone structure to tear heartstrings over, he was breathtaking.

But it was his expression—and what it betrayed of his inner state—that sent tremors radiating through her.

Shaheen wasn't happy. He was deeply dissatisfied,

disturbed. Distraught, even. It might not be apparent to anyone else, but she could sense it as deeply as she felt her own turmoil.

All hope of reprieve, of closure, vanished.

If she'd found him serene, content, she would have been able to move on. But now…

At least there was one thing to be thankful for here. He hadn't seen her. And he wouldn't, if she didn't go through with what she'd planned. And maybe she shouldn't.

No. No maybes about it. Approaching him now would have nothing but terrible consequences. If he had this devastating an effect on her while unaware of her presence and standing thirty feet away, what would he do to her face-to-face?

Infatuated, immature moron that she was, she'd achieved only one thing by seeing him again. She'd compounded her problem and added more heartache to deal with. She could now only curtail further damages.

Cursing herself for a fool, she stepped forward to leave. And felt as if she'd slammed into an impenetrable force field.

Shaheen's gaze.

The impact almost demolished her precarious balance as his eyes bored through her.

She'd always thought they resembled burning coals, even when he'd trained them on her with utmost kindness. But now, with the flare of recognition accompanied by a focus searing in intensity and devoid of gentleness, she felt their burn down to her bones. Her blood started to sizzle, her cheeks to steam.

She'd gravely underestimated the size of the mistake

she'd made coming here. She now had no doubt it was one she'd regret for the rest of her life.

She stood, rooted, mesmerized as he approached her, watching him with the same fatalism one would an out-of-control car on a collision course.

Regret had swamped Shaheen the moment he'd set foot in Aidan's sprawling penthouse. It intensified with every step deeper into the cacophony of forced gaiety.

He shouldn't have agreed to come. He should have told Aidan this wasn't a farewell party to him, but a funeral pyre.

And here was his friend and partner, coming to add to his misery with a blithe smile splitting his face.

"Hey, Sheen!" Aidan exclaimed over the skull-splitting techno music. "I thought you'd decided to let me look like a fool. Again."

Shaheen winced an attempt at a smile. He hated it when his friends abbreviated his name to Sheen. His western friends did so because it was a more familiar name to them, and those back home because that was the first letter of his name in Arabic. He didn't know why he put up with it. But then again, what was a nickname he disliked compared to what he would be forced to endure from now on?

Shaheen peered down into his friend's grinning face, his lips twisting on his barely leashed irritation. "If I'd known what kind of event you were planning, Aidan, I would have."

"You know what they say about all work and no play." Aidan hooked his arm high up around Shaheen's shoulder.

Shaheen almost flinched. He liked the man, and he did come from a culture where physical demonstrations of affection were the norm, contradictorily between members of the same gender. Apart from immediate family, he didn't appreciate being touched. Even in sexual situations, he didn't like women to paw him, as they seemed to unanimously wish to. His liaisons were about taking off an edge, not about intimacy. He'd made that clear, on a take-it-or-leave-it basis, to all the women he'd had such liaisons with.

He could barely remember his last sexual encounter. Such carnal couplings, devoid of any deeper connection, had lost their appeal and begun to grate, to defile. To be expected, he guessed, when the women he liked and respected didn't arouse any carnal inclinations in him.

He stepped away smoothly, severing his friend's embrace without letting him feel the distaste behind the move. "If being dull is the opposite of this…frenzy, I assure you, I prefer it."

A disconcerted expression seeped into Aidan's eyes, replacing the teasing. After six years of business partnership, the man had no idea what Shaheen appreciated. Probably because he kept Aidan, like everyone else, at arm's length. But Aidan had set this up with the best of intentions. And though those usually led to hell, it wasn't fair to show him how wasted his efforts truly were.

He gathered the remnants of his decorum. "But it's not every day I say goodbye to my freedom. So the… fanfare is…" he paused before he forced himself to add "…welcome."

Aidan's face cleared, and his words came out in the rush of the eager to please. "It's not like you'll really lose your freedom. I hear these royal arranged marriages are the epitome of…flexibility." Aidan added that last word with a huge wink and slap on the back.

Shaheen almost snapped his oblivious friend's head off. It was a good thing Aidan turned away from him, exclaiming at the top of his voice to the people who'd flocked over to shake Shaheen's hand.

Shaheen set himself on auto, performing as Aidan wished him to. No point in setting Aidan straight anyway. He wasn't really all there with a few drinks in him. Shaheen should let him wallow in his rare surrender to heedlessness without dragging him into the land of harsh reality where *he* now existed.

His whole existence was about to cave in.

Not on the professional level. There, he'd never stopped soaring from one success to another. But on the personal level, things had been unraveling for a long time. He could even pinpoint the day when it had all started to go downhill. His fight with Aram.

Before that point, he'd lived a carefree existence where he'd felt his future was limitless. But things had gone from bad to worse since then.

He'd long known that, as a prince, he was expected to make a marriage of state, but he'd always shoved that expectation to the back of his mind, hoping that one or both of his older brothers would make a terrific political match. Then Amjad, his oldest brother and crown prince, *had* made such a match. And it had ended in disaster.

Amjad's wife had come to the marriage already pregnant, had schemed to murder Amjad and pass the child as his, to remain forever a princess and the mother of the heir to the throne.

After Amjad had divorced her in a scandal that still resounded in the region, he'd torn through the world acquiring power until he'd become almost as powerful as all of Zohayd put together. No one dared ask him to make another political match. He'd said that, when it was time for him to become king, his brother Harres would be his heir. Failing that, Shaheen. Period.

As for Harres, he would never make a political match, either. It had been agreed that his marriage into any tribe in the region would compromise his position. He'd become the best minister of interior and head of central intelligence and homeland security that Zohayd had ever had, and no one wanted to see the belief in his impartiality tainted. So, if he ever decided to marry—which seemed unlikely, since he hadn't favored any particular woman of the reported hundreds he'd bedded in his thirty-six years—Harres would nevertheless be free to choose his own wife.

So it fell to Shaheen to make a blood-mixing marriage that would revitalize the wavering pacts between factions. He was the last of the king's "pure-blood" sons, born to a purely Zohaydan queen. Haidar and Jalal, Shaheen's half brothers from the current queen, Sondoss, who was Azmaharian, weren't considered pure enough for the unification the marriage was required to achieve.

For years now, he'd known there was no escape from his fate, but instead of becoming resigned to the idea, he'd hated it more daily. It felt like a death sentence hanging over his head.

Only days ago—the day following his thirty-fourth birthday, to be exact—he'd decided to get the suffocating suspense over with, turn himself in to the marriage pact. He'd announced his capitulation to his father, told him to start lining up the bridal candidates. The next day, the news that he was seeking a bride had been all over the media. As one of the most eligible royals in the world, his intention to marry—with the identity of the bride still undecided—was the stuff of the most sensational news.

And here he was, enduring the party his associate was throwing for him to celebrate his impending imprisonment.

He flicked a look at his watch, did a double take. It had been only *minutes.* And he'd shaken a hundred hands and grimaced at double that many artificially elated or intoxicated faces.

Enough. He'd make his excuses to Aidan and bolt from this nightmare. Aidan was probably too far gone to miss him, anyway.

Deciding to do just that, he turned around…and all air left his lungs. Across the room, he saw…*her.*

The jolt of recognition seemed to bring the world to a staggering halt. Everything held its breath as he met her incredible dark eyes across the vast, crowded space.

He stood there for a stretch that couldn't be calculated on a temporal scale, staring at her. Hooks of awareness snapped across the distance and sank into him, flesh and senses, causing animation to screech through him for the first time in over twelve years.

There was no conscious decision to what he did next. A compulsion far beyond his control propelled him in her direction, as if he were hypnotized, remote-controlled.

The crowd parted as if pushed away by the power of his urge. Even the music seemed to observe the significance of the moment as it came to an abrupt stop.

He finally stopped, too, just feet away. He kept that much distance between them so his gaze could sweep her from head to foot.

He devoured his first impressions of her. Gold and bronze locks that gleamed over creamy shoulders and lush breasts encased in deepest chocolate off-the-shoulder taffeta the color of her eyes, the dress nipping in at an impossibly small waist then flaring over softly curved hips into a layered skirt. A face sculpted from exquisiteness, eyes from intelligence and sensitivity, cheeks from inborn class, a nose from daintiness, and lips from passion.

And those were the broad brushstrokes. Then came the endless details. He'd need an hour, a day, to marvel at each.

"Say something." He heard the hunger in his rasp, saw its effect on her.

She shuddered, confusion rising to rival the searing heat in her eyes.

"I..."

Elation bubbled through him. "Yes. You. Say something so that I can believe you're really here."

"I'm... I don't..." She paused, consternation knotting her brow. It only enhanced her beauty.

But he'd heard enough of her rich, velvet voice to know it matched her uniqueness, echoed her perfection.

"You don't know what to say to me? Or you don't know where to start?"

"Shaheen, I..."

She stopped again, and his heart did, too. For at least three heartbeats. He felt almost dizzy, hearing her utter his name.

A finger below her chin tilted her face up to him, to pore into those eyes he felt he'd fallen into whole.

Then he whispered, "You know me?"

Two

He didn't recognize her?

Johara gaped at Shaheen as the realization sank through her, splashed like a rock into her gut.

She should have known that he wouldn't.

Why should he? He'd probably forgotten she existed.

Even if he hadn't, she looked nothing like the fourteen-year-old he'd known.

That was due in part to her own late blooming and in part to her mother's influence. In Zohayd, Jacqueline Nazaryan had always downplayed Johara's looks. Her mother had later told her she'd known that Johara, having inherited her height and luminescent coloring and her father's bone structure and eyes, would become a tall, curvaceous blonde who possessed a paradoxical brand of beauty. And in the brunette, petite-woman–dominated Zohayd, a woman like Johara would be both a prized jewel and a source of endless trouble. If she'd learned to emphasize her looks, she would have become the target of dangerous desires and illicit offers, heaping trouble on her and her father's head. Her mother had left her in Zohayd secure that Johara had no desire and no means of achieving her potential and would continue looking nondescript.

Once she'd joined her mother in France, Jacqueline had encouraged her to showcase her beauty and had done everything she and her fashion-industry colleagues could to help Johara blossom into a woman who knew how to wield what she was told were considerable assets.

As Johara became a successful designer and businesswoman herself, she learned her mother had been right. Most men saw little beyond the face and body they coveted. Several rich and influential men had tried to acquire her as another trophy to bolster their image, another check on their status report. She'd been fully capable of turning them down, without incident so far. Without the repercussions her mother had feared would have accompanied the same rejections in Zohyad.

So yes. She'd been crazy to think Shaheen would recognize her when the lanky, reed-thin duckling he'd known had become a confident, elegant swan.

And here he was. Looking at her without the slightest flicker of recognition. That instant awareness, that flare of delight at the sight of her hadn't been that. It had been…

What had it been? What was that she saw playing on his lips, blazing in his eyes as he inclined his awesome head at her? What was it she felt electrocuting her from his fingers, still caressing her chin? Was it possible he…?

"Of course you know who I am." Shaheen cut through her feverish contemplations, shook his head in self-deprecation. The flashes from the mirror balls and revolving disco lights shot sparks of copper off the luxury of his mane and into the fathomless translucence of his eyes, zapping her into ever-deepening paralysis. "You're attending my farewell party, after all."

She remained mute. He thought she recognized him only because he was a celebrity in whose name he thought she was here having free drinks and an unrepeatable networking opportunity.

He relinquished her chin only to let the back of his fingers travel in a gossamer up-down stroke over her almost combusting cheek. "So to whom should I offer my unending thanks for inviting you here?"

Her heart constricted as the reality of the situation crystallized.

She hadn't even factored in that he might not know her on sight. But she'd conceded she shouldn't have expected it. But that there was nothing about her that jogged any sense of familiarity in him—that she couldn't rationalize. Or accept.

Her insides compacted in a tight tangle of disappointment.

His words and actions so far had had nothing to do with happiness at seeing her after all these years. There was only one reason he could have approached her, was talking to her, looking at her this way. It seemed absurd, unthinkable. But she could find no other explanation.

Shaheen was coming on to her.

As if he'd heard her thoughts, he seemed to tighten all of his virility and influence around her, dropping his voice an octave, sinking it right through to her core. "This will sound like the oldest line in the book, but even though you haven't said one complete sentence to me yet and we met just minutes ago, I feel like I've known you forever."

The music chose that second to blare again, as if accentuating his announcement, cutting off any possibility of her blurting out that he felt that way because he had.

At the deafening intrusion, he dropped his hand from her cheek, raised his head, his eyes releasing hers from their snare as he cast an annoyed look at the whole scene. He caught her again with the full force of his focus a moment later. "This place is incompatible with human sanity." His eyes forged another path of fire down her body to where her purse was hanging limply from her hand. "I see you've got your bag with you. Shall we go?"

She gasped as currents forked through her from where his hand curved around her upper arm in courteous yet compelling invitation. "B-but it's your party."

His eyes crinkled at her as his lips spread, revealing the even power of his teeth. "*Aih,* and I'll leave if I want to." His thumb swept the naked flesh of her arm, causing a firestorm to ripple through her as though through a wheat field in a storm. "And how I want to."

Her free fist came up, pressing against a heart that seemed to be trying to ram out of her chest cavity.

The world had always transformed into a wonderland when he smiled. But this was…ridiculous. There should be a law against his indulging in the practice in inhabited areas!

She blinked, her sluggish gaze drifting from his at the pull of something vague. And she blinked again. In disbelief.

She was no longer in the middle of the party. She was in a spacious marble hall, walking on jellified legs toward what she judged to be McCormick's private elevator.

Had she really walked here? Or had he teleported them?

Suddenly it was all too much. His every move and glance stripping her of basic coherence, his very nearness inching her to the verge of collapse as she and the situation spiraled out of control. He didn't have the slightest memory of her, was enacting this aggressive seduction based on her anonymity, confident of her availability.

Still, only when they stopped in front of the elevator did she manage to attempt to extract herself smoothly from his loose yet incapacitating grip. Her spinning senses made her stumble back instead, wrenching her arm away.

She could see astonishment reverberate through him as the spectacular wings of his eyebrows snapped together and his lips lost the fullness of intimacy, chiseling into harsher lines that accentuated their perfection. And showed her yet another side of him that she'd never been exposed to—the ruthless royal he could become when provoked or displeased.

So he couldn't comprehend that a female would have the temerity to not fall all over herself to obey his decrees? Maybe this encounter would end in closure, after all. Just in a different way than she'd imagined.

She glared her disillusion up into his eyes. "You're so certain I want to leave with you, aren't you?"

Bitterness hardened her voice. She knew he heard it loud and clear, too.

The last of the heat in his gaze drained as stillness descended. "Yes, I am. As certain of my desire to leave with you."

She huffed her fury. "You're right. You *are* spouting the oldest lines in the book."

His pupils expanded, almost engulfed his vivid irises. "I realize they sound like that, but they happen to be true."

Her lips twisted, mimicking a fiercer contortion of her heart. "Sure they are."

"You think I'm so lacking in imagination or finesse that I'd use something so hackneyed to express myself if it wasn't the simple truth, and no other words would do?"

"Maybe you're just too lazy, too jaded to think of something new. Or you can't even fathom the possibility that you might need a new line. Or maybe you didn't think I warranted the effort of coming up with something a tad more original, since you thought I'd fall flat on my back at the idea of your interest."

He seemed more taken aback at every word firing from her lips, his scowl dissolving into a flabbergasted look.

She was as shocked as he was. Where had all that come from? It was as if pressure had been building up inside her, and disappointment was a blade that had slashed across the thin membrane holding it in, her feelings bursting out of containment.

She'd just loved him for so long!

She'd fantasized about how it would be if they met again, and reality had demolished every comforting scenario. His indiscriminating carnal purpose made a mockery of the soul-deep connection she'd been convinced they'd resurrect on sight. A connection, it seemed, that existed only inside her lovesick mind.

The insupportable deduction squeezed more resentment from her depths. "And didn't it occur to you that the person you felt you owed unending thanks to for bringing me here might be my boyfriend, or even my fiancé or husband?"

All expression evaporated, leaving his face a hard mask. "No. It didn't."

"It didn't, or the possibility of my being committed to another man didn't seem relevant to you?"

"You *can't* be. I would have felt something, from you, a connection with someone else, a disconnection from me. But—"

He stopped abruptly. That limitless energy that had radiated from him from the moment he'd caught her eye flickered, wavered. Then it blinked out. The gloom she'd thought she'd seen tainting his aura before he'd noticed her descended on him again like a roiling thundercloud, seeming to slump his formidable shoulders under its weight.

He closed his eyes, swept a palm over his eyes and forehead. His other hand joined in, raking up through his hair before rubbing down his face.

Then he let his hands drop to his sides, leveled his eyes at hers. The bleakness there shriveled her insides.

"I don't know what came over me. I saw you across the room and I thought... No, I didn't think. I *knew.* I was certain you looked at me with the same...recognition. That sense I've heard people experience when they meet someone who's...right. It must have been a trick of the lights. Your recognition was of the literal variety, and I saw what I subconsciously wanted to see. I must be in worse shape than even I thought, imagining I'd found an undeniable connection at such a party. Or at all. I apologize. To you, and to your man. I should have known you'd be taken."

His fists clenched and unclenched as he spoke, as if

they itched with the same sick electricity discharging inside her limbs. Then with a shake of his head and an indecipherable imprecation, he turned away.

She stood feeling as if she'd been struck by lightning, watching his long strides take him away from her. All she could think was that he didn't seem callous or indiscriminating, only hurt, and that the last thing she'd ever see of him was that look of despondency on his face.

"It was a hypothetical question."

At her squeaking statement, he stopped. But didn't turn. He only inclined his face so that she saw his profile, eyes cast downward, tension emanating from him in shockwaves.

She forced the explanation he was waiting for between barely working lips. "When I mentioned a boyfriend or fiancé or husband, it was only in a 'what if' scenario. I don't have anyone."

"You're not taken." His hoarse whisper shuddered through her as he turned toward her, animation creeping back into his face. She shook her head, had locks snaring in her trembling mouth. "You objected to me sweeping you away because—" he accentuated every other word with a leisurely step back to her side, each hitting her like a seismic wave "—you mistook me for a lazy, jaded oaf who doesn't possess an original bone in his body to express his inability to wait to be alone with you, or a poetic cell with which to do justice to the wonder of our meeting."

She was panting as he fell silent. "Okay, I hereby revise my opinion. You have nothing but original bones and poetic cells."

The elation reclaiming his expression spiked on a guffaw. Her knees almost buckled. And that was before a hunger-laden step obliterated the last of the distance between them. Every hair on her body stood on end as if with a giant static charge.

Then he whispered, "Tell me you feel it, too. Tell me the almost tangible entity I sense between us exists, that I'm not having a breakdown and imagining things."

This was the second time he'd alluded to his condition. The idea of his suffering spread thorns in her chest. She bit her lip on the pain. "The…entity exists."

"I am going to touch you now. Will you shake me off again, or do you want me to?" She shook her head, nodded, groaned. Her teeth would start clattering any moment now with needing his touch.

He took both her arms in the warm gentleness of his hands. Then he pulled her to him. She stumbled forward, ended up with her head where she'd dreamed of having it since she'd been old enough to form memories. Where it had rested once before, during that moment that had changed her destiny. On the endlessness of his chest. He pressed it there with a hand that smoothed her hair, his rumbling purr of enjoyment echoing her own.

He finally sighed. "This is unprecedented. We've had our first fight and reconciliation before you've even told me your name."

"It wasn't really a fight," she whispered as she pulled back a bit, so she could breathe, so her heart wouldn't stop.

He smiled down at her, his eyes telling her she delighted him. "Not on my end, but you were about to claw my eyes out. And I would have gladly let you. But I'm not putting it off any longer. Your name, *ya ajaml makhloogah fel kone*. Bless me with its gift."

He'd just called her the most beautiful creature in the universe. He probably didn't realize he had spoken in his native tongue, or he would have tagged it with a translation.

"J…" Her voice vanished on a convulsive swallow as he drew nearer still, as if to inhale her name when she uttered it like the most pleasurable fragrance, like life-sustaining air.

And she realized she couldn't tell him who she was.

If she did, he'd pull back. There would be embarrassment, consternation followed by distance and decorum. And she couldn't bear to lose this moment of spontaneity with him.

It would be the last thing she had of him.

"Gemma."

She almost slapped herself upside the head. Gemma? Did she have to go for a literal translation? How obvious could she get?

But then, she'd started to say her name, and he would have thought it suspicious if she'd gone on to say Dana or Sara or something. Gemma had been the only name that had come to her that started with a *J* sound.

Before she made it worse, she had to tell him how nice it was to meet him and walk away. *Run* away. Without looking back. She had the rest of her life to look back on this magical encounter.

He thwarted her feverish plans, pressed her head closer as he sighed his contentment. "Gemma. Perfect, *ya joharti.*" She lurched at hearing her real name. Before she could have a heart attack, he loosened his embrace, smiled his pleasure. "That's 'my jewel' in my mother tongue. So, my precious Gemma, will you come with me?"

"Where?" she choked.

"As long as you're with me, does it matter?"

* * *

It was clear by now that nothing mattered.

Not to Johara. Not when measured against wringing this opportunity to be with Shaheen of its last possible glance and smile, touch and comeback. Of the sheer unbridled joy of being the object of his interest, the target of his appreciation, the instigator of his desire.

Another breaker of pleasure frothed inside her as she beheld him, a vision made man, sitting across from her in the exclusive restaurant he'd made literally so for their dinner.

They'd been talking nonstop since they'd left McCormick's penthouse. She'd answered his questions about herself without specifying names or places, and nothing she told him had rung any bells. That still rankled, but her thankfulness for this time out of time his unawareness afforded her with him surpassed any disappointment.

"Do you want to know what the maitre d' told me after emptying the restaurant?" His eyes glittered at her as his hand covered her upturned palm with hypnotic strokes. "That such heavy-handed tactics wouldn't work on a lady of such refinement as you."

She giggled, surrendered her hand to his possession. "A very astute gentleman."

He gave an exaggerated sigh. "I wish you had told me that before *he* emptied half of my supposed no-limit credit card."

She giggled again at his mock woe. Even in her upheaval, the thrill rose. Her fantasies throughout the years had gotten it right. Their connection *was* there. And he was showering her with the delighted, delighting banter that had always textured and colored her life.

He remained the man she'd loved since she could

remember. No, he was better than that man. Much, much better.

She sighed at the bittersweetness of it all. "But seriously, you shouldn't have gone to any expense. I thought we'd agreed it didn't matter where we were."

"I wanted to be alone with you."

"We could have been alone walking down the pier."

"That did occur to me, but you're not dressed for the cold night." He lowered his gaze as if pondering the pattern he was painting with his fingers on her palm. He raised his eyes a moment later and she gasped. Gentleness and humor were gone, that grim god of the desert back. She shuddered with the fierceness of her response. "You know where I really want to be alone with you, Gemma. In my place. In my bed."

She squeezed her eyelids shut as emotion tore through her.

She couldn't handle this. She shouldn't have sought him out…

His tough rider's fingers smoothed over her eyes, making her open them, so that there was no escaping his fierceness, his intention. "I want you, Gemma. I never knew wanting like this existed, that I could feel anything of this intensity and purity."

"Purity?"

"Yes. It's unclouded, untainted, absolute. I want you, in every way. And you want me in the same way. I know I wouldn't be feeling like this if you didn't also. My desire surges from me as much as it stems from you. It flows to you and is reflected back at me exponentially, then back to you in a never-ending cycle. It's taking on a life of its own, growing too powerful to deny. With every breath its power heightens, sharpens. Will you let me fulfill our desire? Will you let me worship you?"

"Shaheen, please—"

He suddenly pushed his chair back, stood up. Before her heart could stumble on its next beat, he was bending to pluck her from her chair and into his arms. Her head lolled back over his arm with shock as he tightened his hold behind her back, beneath her knees and buried his lips in the neck she exposed to him. "This is all I want to do. Please you. I never want to stop pleasing you."

Voices yelled inside her head. *Tell him who you are. He'll stop this torment the moment he realizes your identity.*

And he'd be furious with her for hiding it. She couldn't let it end like that. With him feeling deceived. And hating her.

She had to say no. He'd abide by her refusal. She hadn't meant for any of this to happen. From the moment he'd caught her eyes and zapped her control across the room, she'd been reacting without volition.

Then she opened her mouth and without any trace of it she whispered, "Yes. Please."

Three

Johara hadn't known what to expect when she'd said yes to Shaheen.

It certainly hadn't been anything that had happened in the two hours since.

After he swept her into his arms and obtained her unconditional capitulation, he put her down, let her walk out of the restaurant and to his limo. He gave his driver an order in Arabic to take the most roundabout way home then sat beside her talking, about everything under the sun. All through the long drive to his penthouse, he didn't touch her at all, except for resuming his thorough fascination with her hand.

For a stretch, he showed her family photos on his phone. He had a few of his father and brothers. They looked much like she remembered, just older and harsher towering specimens of manhood. But the photos were mostly of his aunt Bahiyah, his half sister, Aliyah, and his cousin, Laylah, the only three females born in their family in five generations straight. Shaheen said they were the only ones worth taking and keeping photos of, the vivacious centerpieces of their all-male family, splashes of beauty and grace and exuberance among the range of darkness and drive of what the ladies called their testosterone-compromised relatives.

Aliyah, who was three years older than Johara and who'd seldom been around in the eight years Johara had lived in the palace, had been thought to be King Atef's niece. It was only two years ago that it had been revealed that Princess Bahiyah had adopted her and passed her off as hers from her American husband, when she was actually the king's daughter from an American lover. Instead of causing a scandal, the discovery had aborted the looming wars in the region when Aliyah entered a political marriage with the new king of Judar, Kamal Aal Masood.

Aliyah looked nothing like the sallow, spaced-out girl she remembered. In fact, she looked the epitome of femininity and elegance. And bliss. It was apparent her forced marriage to Kamal had become a love match. Like Shaheen's impending marriage would no doubt become. For what woman wouldn't worship him?

She blinked away the mist of dejection and concentrated on Laylah's photos. The twelve-year old girl she'd been when Johara had last seen her had fulfilled all the promise she'd shown of becoming a spectacular beauty. Johara had never had a chance to really know her, since Laylah's mother, Queen Sondoss's sister, had never let her mingle with the help, as Aram had put it.

Shaheen said Laylah was one of three reasons he forgave his stepmother for existing, since she'd married her sister to his uncle, the other two being his half brothers, Haidar and Jalal. He also said that the ladies reveled in giving their male family members—especially Shaheen and his brothers—a view of a life that didn't have to bend to their wishes. Because of that, along with many other things he could see they shared with Johara, he was certain they would set the palace on fire getting along.

Everything he said alluded to his taking it for granted that her presence in his life would continue beyond tonight. But he must know there was no chance of that.

Yet not only had he already secured her surrender, so he had no reason to say anything more to encourage it, he seemed to believe in what he was saying, to have forgotten the marriage of state he'd announced his intention to enter only four days ago.

She guessed that the marriage was what had been weighing so heavily on him when she'd first seen him. He was loathe to succumb to duty. But it seemed to have slipped his mind since he'd seen her.

She wouldn't remind him. They'd both remember harsh reality soon enough, live with it for the rest of their lives.

Tonight was theirs.

So here she was, standing in the middle of his extensive, austerely masculine foyer, watching him as he hung his jacket and her wrap with tranquil, precise movements.

Why was he wasting their precious time together?

She might not have known what to expect, but she'd thought he'd escalate the urgency he'd shown so far. She'd had visions of him carrying her to the limo, drowning her in kisses all the way here, pressing her against the door the moment they entered and showing her how eager for her he was.

Had he remembered his commitments and decided to cool things off, let her down easy?

She should spare him the discomfort, should leave. She shouldn't have come at all, shouldn't have said yes, shouldn't have gone to that party…

Something whirred, flashed. She blinked in surprise, her left eye riddled in blue spots.

He'd snapped a photo of her with his phone. Now he walked toward her, big and lithe, gloriously male and impossibly beautiful. But it was his expression that made her sway, sending her heart swinging in her chest like a pendulum.

The lightness of the trek here was gone, sizzling sensuality replacing it, setting his eyes deeper on fire and his charisma to a higher level.

He stopped a foot away, reached for the hands he seemed so enamored with. "You looked so…pensive. And if possible, even more breathtaking. This photo is the stuff of the immortal masterpieces the old masters would have begged to portray." He took her hands to his lips, giving each finger a knuckle-by-knuckle introduction to the cosseting of his lips, his eyes empty of all but seriousness. "Are you having second thoughts?"

"No." The denial shot out of her, its fierceness mortifying her as it rang around them. But she had to know. "A-are you?"

He huffed. "The only thoughts I'm having are where to begin worshipping you and how to stop from swallowing you whole."

So that was why he was holding back. He feared being too aggressive. She was being insecure again.

But who could blame her? All through the years, her love for him had been emotional, spiritual, with slight sensual overtones. She'd never imagined he could actually want her, and when she'd fantasized that he did, even in the freedom of her own imagination, he'd done no more than hold and kiss her. Yet she couldn't breathe with wanting all he was willing to give her, with needing to experience him to the fullest.

She swayed closer, her heartbeats merging like the wings of a hummingbird with the enormity of what she was feeling, what she was about to reveal. "B-begin anywhere, Shaheen. J-just begin. And don't stop yourself. I don't want you to stop."

His eyes flared with her every faltering word. When she fell into embarrassed, panting silence, he entwined her hands in his, brought them to her face, twisting their embrace around so the backs of his hands stroked up and down her flaming cheeks.

"Then I'll begin here. Your skin. It's incredible, like every part of you. Lush, thick cream, free of paleness and fragility. It doesn't flush with your emotions, no matter how strong, only becomes more vital, more vivid. It's glowing now. Your eyes are gleaming like polished onyxes under spotlights, inundating me with an avalanche of expressions, each intoxicating in its clarity and beauty. And your lips. The way they mold to your every thought, the way they take the shape of your every emotion, the way they tremble to the frequency of each sensation…each tremor shudders through me until I am nothing but uncontainable hunger."

She almost choked with stimulation. "I was right. You are made up of nothing but original bones and poetic cells."

His lips twitched in a lethal mix of appreciation and

predation as he touched the pad of his thumb to hers, stilling those tremors that so affected him. "It seems you didn't hear my last words clearly."

Her lips trembled even more as humor warred with anticipation and agitation. He rubbed his thumbs against them, his breathing becoming harsher.

She closed her eyes to savor the long-dreamed-about sensations. Her wildest imaginings hadn't prepared her for reality. She moaned with the pleasure that corkscrewed through her, emanating from his breath, his nearness, his touch, to her every inch, her deepest reaches. Then her lips did what they'd been longing to do for most of her life—caressed the fragrant warmth and power pressed to them with a trembling kiss.

She heard his intake of breath. It sliced away more of the leashes of her inhibition. She opened her lips, grazed her teeth against his skin. Its texture, its scent, brought more moist heat surging from her core.

A fiercer inhalation expanded his chest until it pressed against her swelling breasts. She knew he could scent her arousal, felt the wildness it sent seething through him. It made her light-headed, the knowledge that she could do this to him, that he was doing this to her, that they had this to share.

Feeling bolder, she swept her tongue against his skin. Her knees did buckle at her first taste of him. He disentangled his other hand, caught her around the waist. She kept her eyes closed as she dove deeper into the sensations, her whole existence centering on his thumb against her tongue as he began to thrust it gently in and out of her mouth.

"This is extremely dangerous." His bass hiss made her eyes snap open. His bore into them before moving to her lips with burning intent as he fed them his thumb, as they suckled it with increasing greed and abandon. She knew what he meant. He still elaborated. "That you want me as fiercely as I want you."

She nodded, breath leaving her body under choppy pressure. She felt she was disintegrating with need for him.

He let go of her waist, grazed across her lower teeth as he slid his thumb lingeringly from between her lips, then dropped his forehead to hers, nuzzling her, inhaling her. "This is unparalleled. Agonizing but sublime."

"Yes," she whispered.

Though she had no experience to back up her belief, she knew the protracted inflammation of their senses was far more satisfying than any frenzied mindless coupling would be.

He eased her away only to glide both arms around her back, to her dress's zipper. He slid it down with torturous slowness, never letting go of her eyes as he went back up to unclasp her bra. She gasped as its constriction eased, and again at the spike of ferocity in his eyes as he monitored her reaction. He drew more gasps from her as he caressed her dress and bra loose, then in one silky sweep, freed her from their shackles.

Before she could snap her arms across her nakedness, he dragged her dress beyond her waist to her hips, dropping downward with it. He ended up on his knees before her.

Her mouth opened, closed, opened again. From unbearable stimulation. From the way he looked her up and down, as if he would truly gobble her up.

Then he pulled her to him, rumbling, "Now, I worship you."

She would have keeled over him if his shoulders hadn't stopped her forward pitch. He added to her imbalance, burying hot lips into her flesh. She whimpered at each press into her abdomen, every tongue thrust into her navel, each tooth drag across her breasts. Her moans sharpened as he gently clamped her nipples, until a cry rushed out at his first hard pull. "Shaheen...*please*."

In answer, he bunched her skirt in his hands, his thumbs hooking into the top of her panties. Then, in one magical move, every shred of covering was shed off of her.

Standing in nothing but her shoes with her clothes pooled at her feet, she felt the world recede. Shaheen looked up, the worshipping he'd promised her setting the hard nobility of his face ablaze.

This was beyond unprecedented. Beyond unparalleled. *She was with Shaheen.* Standing before him naked. She was about to be his in the flesh, just as she was already his in every other way.

She watched as he raised each leg to kiss and fondle from calf to thigh, her consciousness flickering like a bulb about to short out. She heard his magnificent voice as he raggedly lavished far better than poetry on her, spontaneous wonder pouring out in whatever language expressed it best.

She moaned constantly, becoming a literal puddle of arousal by the time he rose. She would have collapsed at his feet if he hadn't swept her up as he stood.

When she flopped in his arms like a ragdoll, he whispered into her ear, "Wrap yourself around me, my Gemma. Cling to me with all of your priceless flesh and desire."

That injected power into her limp muscles. She wanted to. *He* wanted her to. She only ever wished to give him what he wanted.

She clasped her arms around his shoulders, her thighs

around his hips. And it was indescribable. Feeling all of his heat and bulk and power and arousal encased within her limbs, being draped around all of that. She'd be forever empty and anchorless when she no longer had him to enfold, to hang on to like this.

But she had him now.

She rested her head against his shoulder as he strode across his penthouse with her clasped in his arms. Her eyes remained open, but she registered only impressions of his character, his taste and wealth imbuing the spaces, all the more impressive for being unpretentious. Then he crossed into a bedroom. His bedroom.

This was the last thing she'd expected would happen when she'd embarked upon her mission to see him one last time. That she'd end up in his bedroom. In his bed.

But she wanted to be here more than literally anything.

Her senses revved out of their stupor. This was where he slept, where he woke up, where he read and showered and shaved, where he dressed and undressed. Where he pleasured himself. And where she was convinced he'd never pleasured another.

This was his sanctum, when he lived in New York. And he was giving her the exclusive privilege of being here. It would be a one-time pass. She had to make all she could of it.

The huge, high-ceilinged room was lit with only a bedside lamp. Her gaze, avid to soak in more of his privacies and secrets, had just registered the slashes of bold décor, gradations of dark grays and greens with accents of hardwood the color of his eyes when her wandering ones came to a hiccupping halt.

He pressed her against the door as she'd vaguely

hoped he would before, held her there with only his bulk bearing down on her.

She shuddered at the sensory overload. The coolness of the polished wood against her back, the feel of him pressing against her, the heat and hardness of his erection against her intimate flesh with nothing but his clothes between them.

Until minutes ago she'd been too shy to inspect his arousal. Even now she couldn't make the leap of imagining anything beyond this. Her mind almost shut down at the thought of having him inside her. And he hadn't even kissed her on the lips yet....

He raised his head from razing his way down her throat. "And now, I pleasure you, *ya galbi.*"

Hearing him call her "my heart" tore a sob from her depths.

He frowned at the sound. "Gemma, if you want me to stop, I will. If you're not totally sure..."

She dragged his head down to her, took the kiss she'd been starving for all of her life.

He stilled under her uncoordinated frenzy, let her smash her lips against his, imploring his reciprocation, his taking over, before he wrenched his lips away.

"What's wrong, my Gemma?" He swept her around, took her to the bed, laid her down on it, where the lighting afforded him the best view of her. And he jerked up in dismay. "You're crying!"

Her hands flailed over his shoulders, trying to drag him back to her. "I-I'm not...I just want you, too much. I can't wait anymore. Please take me, Shaheen. T-take me now."

The concern on his face dissipated, sheer ferocity slamming down in its place. "I want to take you. I want to invade you and ride you until you weep with pleasure this time. But I can't. I have to ready you for me first or I'll hurt you."

"You won't. I'm ready. Just…just…"

"*Galbi,* let me pace this. I need to make it perfect for you."

"It will be perfect. Anything with you is perfect."

He growled something as he dragged her onto his lap. "Don't say one more word, Gemma. If you don't want to have a raving lunatic all over you. I've never even imagined being out of control. But I am now."

She sobbed a giggle. "If this is you out of control, I'd hate to see you in it. You'd probably kill me with frustration."

This time it was his lips that stopped her words, in that kiss she'd imagined since she was old enough to know what kisses were. It turned out she'd never even come close to knowing.

This was a kiss. This tender ferociousness. This gentle devouring. Only this. Shaheen possessing her lips, each sweep and pull and thrust layering sensations, burying her in pleasure. His scent and taste and feel filling her, his hunger finishing her.

She undulated beneath him, until he subdued her, held her arms above her head as his other hand flowed down from her face to her shoulder, ending up cupping the aching heaviness of one breast. "You're only allowed to moan for more, and cry out with pleasure. That will be enough to drive me out of my mind."

"Let me see you," she moaned.

"Not yet. And you're already breaking the rules."

"You said I could moan for more. I am, for more of you."

"You'll have all of me, every way you like. Just not now."

"You're being unfair," she whimpered.

"It's you who's unfair. Nothing should be this magnificent."

She tried to free her hands. She needed them on him, any part of him, without the barrier of clothes.

He growled deep in his chest, spread her back and continued owning her body with his sensual torment. But it was only when he slid her hips to the edge of the bed and kneeled before her again that she realized his intention. Her heart stuttered.

It was stupid to feel embarrassed at having his mouth and hands on her intimate flesh when she was begging for far more. But there it was. She tried to close her legs.

He insisted, caressed them apart. "Open yourself to me, let me feast on you. Let me prepare you."

"I'm prepared," she cried out. "Please!"

"I don't want to hold back when I take you, and only a few climaxes will prepare you for my possession."

"A *few...?*" She choked on incredulity.

What was he going to do to her?

Anything. She'd take anything and everything he did to her.

She opened herself to him and those long, perfect fingers caressed her feminine lips apart, slid through her molten need. She keened, lurched with jolts of sensation almost too much to bear. And that was before he dipped one finger in. Each slow inch felt like pure pleasure. It made her realize how empty she'd felt. How only having him inside her would fill the void.

She tried to drag him up to her with her legs. He only opened her fully and burned her to the core in his ragged hunger.

She malfunctioned completely as his magnificent head settled between her thighs and his lips and tongue scorched the heart of her femininity. The sight, the concept of what he was doing to her, giving her, was almost more incapacitating than the physical sensations.

Through the delirium, she watched him cosset her, strum her, drink her, revel in her essence, in her need and taste and pleasure. He seemed to know when she couldn't take any more.

"Now, *ya roh galbi,* let me see and hear how much I pleasure you." Then his tongue swept her flesh again.

Her body unraveled in a chain-reaction of convulsions, in soul-racking ecstasy, as she held his eyes all through, letting him see what he was doing to her.

She subsided, unable even to beg him to come to her, and he began again, varying his method, renewing her desperation, deepening her surrender.

She'd lost count of how many times he'd wrung her pleasure when at one point he kept her on the brink, came up to straddle her.

He painted her with caresses, kneaded her breasts, gently squeezed her nipples. "I've never seen or tasted anything so beautiful."

Her hands shook on his belt, trying to undo it. "I want to see you—all of you. I want you, inside me, filling my body. Please, Shaheen, please *now.*"

He surged up to stand over the bed, over her, stripping off his clothes with barely leashed violence and absolute economy.

Though she was dying for him, the one opportunity she'd have to see his exposed glory took precedence. She swayed to her knees, gaping at his proportionate perfection, the rippling power encased in polished bronze and accentuated with dark silk.

With a cry she surged forward, her hands and lips

seeking all she could reach of him, wanting them everywhere at once.

"Shaheen..." she moaned between kisses "...you're more beautiful than I imagined...I want to worship each inch of you, too."

He threaded his fingers through her hair. "Later, *ya hayati,* we'll worship each other inch for inch. Now I take you. And you take me."

"Yes." She fell to her back, held out her arms.

He surged to her, covered her. She cried out, reveling in how her softness cushioned his hardness.

Perfect. No, sublime. Like he'd said.

She opened her legs, as she'd always opened everything she was to him. He guided them over his waist, his eyes seeking hers, solicitous and tempestuous, his erection seeking her entrance.

Finding both hot and molten, he growled his surrender at last, sank into her in one forceful thrust.

She'd been certain it wouldn't hurt, that she was ready.

But she couldn't have been ready for this. For him.

And it wasn't only her untried body. She was sure experience wouldn't have helped her withstand the first invasion of his girth and length.

It was on the second thrust that he seemed to realize. Why the first had taken such force, found such resistance, why her cry had been so sharp, why her body was so tense and trembling.

He froze. Shock rippled over his face. At last he choked out, "You're a *virgin?*"

"It's okay...I'm okay. Don't stop...please, Shaheen, don't stop."

"B'Ellahi!" he rasped, tried to pull out of her.

She clamped her quaking legs over his hips, stopping him from exiting her body.

"Stop, Gemma!" he growled, resisting her. "I'm hurting you."

"Yes." This made him heave up, his eyes horrified. She only clung harder to him, arms and legs and core. "And the pain is nothing compared to how you feel inside me, is making it all the more…intense. I feel you…branding me. Please…you said you wouldn't hold back."

"This was before I knew you were…!" He shook his head, his disbelief and bewilderment rising. "*Ya Ullah,* I'm your *first.*"

"Are you…disappointed?"

"Disappointed? Try flabbergasted, overwhelmed. *Ya Ullah.*"

Mortification flooded her. Her limbs relinquished their hold on him. "I should have told you. It wasn't a conscious decision not to…but you have no reason to believe that…" She swallowed the weeping jag that was building behind the barrier of her throat. "Let me up. I'll go and you'll never—"

He slid deeper into her, gentler, slower, his eyes heating again. "Does this feel like I'm sorry I'm your first? I already knew you were the biggest gift I'd ever received. But now you've bestowed this on me, and the gift is even bigger. I wish I could offer you something of the same magnitude."

"You *are* giving me the biggest gift, too." Tears were overtaking her. And that would spoil everything. Her lips trembled with what she hoped approximated teasing. "Figuratively *and* literally." He inhaled sharply, grew even bigger inside her. Even through the burning, she thrust her hips upward, engulfing more of his erection. "So if you really want to give me a gift, don't hold back. Give me all of you."

"You do want a raving lunatic all over you, don't you?"

"Oh, yes, please."

"You say, yes, please, and everything insides me snaps," he growled as he rose, cupped her hips in his hands, tilted her and thrust himself to the hilt inside her. It was overwhelming, being stretched by him, being full of him, beyond her capacity.

He withdrew, and she cried out at the loss, urged him to sink back into her. He resisted her squirming pleas for a moment, his shaft resting at her entrance before he sank slowly back inside her.

She cried out a hot gust of passion, opening wider for him. He watched her, gauging her reactions, adjusting his movements to her every gasp and grimace, waiting for the pleasure to submerge the pain before he let her really have all of him, before he quickened his pace. All through, he kept her at fever pitch, caressing her all over, suckling her breasts, draining her lips, raining wonder over her.

Then he groaned into her lips, "Glorious, *ya galbi,* inside and out, literally and figuratively. Everything about you, with you."

She keened as her depths started to ripple around him. As if he knew, he tilted her, angled his thrusts, and snapped the coil of tension inside her. Convulsion after convulsion squeezed shrieks out of her, clamped her tight around him, inside and out.

Only then did he let go, a moment she'd replay in her memory forever. The sight and feel of him as he surrendered inside her to the ecstasy that union with her brought him. She peaked again as he threw his head back on a roar of pleasure, as the heat of his release surged into her womb until she felt filled, never to be empty again.

Shaking with aftershocks, she whimpered as he moved, needing him to come down on top of her. He swept her around instead, took her over him, careful not to jar her, to remain inside her.

She lay on top of him, the biggest part of her soul, satiated in ways she couldn't have imagined, in perfect peace for the first time in her life.

As he encompassed her in caresses and murmurs of appreciation, awe overtook her at everything that had happened tonight.

Then he made it infinitely better.

He shifted, brought her to her side facing him, kissed her deeply, leisurely, then whispered into her lips, "This was, hands down, the best thing that has ever happened to me. *You* are."

She believed he meant it.

But he wasn't free to mean it.

The knowledge expanded inside her soaring heart, a ton of dejection bringing it crashing to the ground of reality.

But she still had the rest of tonight with him.

Shaking off despondence, she focused on the miracle in progress, in her arms.

She suckled the tongue rubbing against hers, caressed the muscled back rippling beneath her fingers, smiled into his kiss. "Your feelings, sir, are a mere reflection of mine."

He pulled back to look down at her, his own smile bliss and bedevilment at once as he pressed her buttocks closer, driving his intact arousal deeper into her. "Then it's up to me to prove to you how authentic my feelings are."

And for the rest of the night, he left her in no doubt.

Johara drank in the magnificent sight Shaheen made.

Sprawled on his back, the dark green cotton sheet twisted around one thigh and leaving the rest of him bare for her to devour, he had one muscled arm arced over his head, the other with its palm flat over his heart. He looked as if he were holding the kisses she'd planted there before she'd left his side, telling him she'd go to the bathroom and would be back in moments, in place.

Her heart constricted. Her vision blurred.

And she choked out her pledge. "I will always love you, *ya habibi.*"

He sighed in his sleep, his lips curving in contentment.

Even though she was across the room, she thought he said, "I love you, too, my Gemma."

Tears poured thicker, as if they were flowing from her heart. She closed the door and walked away from his room and out of his penthouse. Out of his life.

She felt as if hers was over.

Four

The moment he opened his eyes, Shaheen knew something was wrong. Wonderfully wrong.

He was…serene.

He remained still, closed his eyes again, to savor the alien sensation of absolute contentment.

Yes. Alien. He'd never felt like this, even on his best days.

He'd always been aware of all he had to be thankful for, had never taken any of his privileges for granted. He'd accepted the prices he had to pay for them, had even considered the payments and the load they placed on his shoulders more privileges. He'd reveled in all the challenges and hardships that making use of those privileges had dictated.

What he'd never been as fond of were the constraints they placed on his choices, the frustration he encountered when bowing to their demands meant doing less than what he thought was right.

Usually he relegated those limitations to the back of his mind, but they were still there, a source of constant tension.

There was not a trace of that now. He felt something he'd only ever experienced partially, had never imagined feeling in full. Peace. Permeating. Absolute.

And it was because of her.

Gemma. Even her name was perfection. Everything he'd felt from her, seen of her, had with her had been that. And the wonder of it seemed to have wiped him clean of all that had come before her. That he had to exert conscious effort to remember anything but her was amazing. One night with her felt like the sum total of his experience in life.

He stretched, humming to the tune of satisfaction and elation that strummed through him.

So this was *passion*. He hadn't felt anything like it before. He'd known passion for commitment, for success, for details, he felt love for his family, had felt mild and ephemeral interest in some women. But he'd never imagined anything so encompassing, so consuming. From the moment he'd laid eyes on her, his feelings had engulfed him whole, had overwhelmed his reason and control. Not that what he felt went against either. She satisfied the first and he felt no need to employ the second. Being with her had emptied him of tension and inhibition, had freed him to focus his all on the wonder of being with her, experiencing her, savoring every moment with her.

He did feel he'd known her all his life.

And now he couldn't imagine his life without her. The life she'd derailed. And righted.

He sighed deeply as images and sensations of the previous night and early morning cascaded through his mind and body.

He *had* taken her as if he'd been craving her all his life. He hadn't even been able to stop when he'd found he'd been her first. Or later, when he'd told himself he wouldn't do it again that night. But she'd again hijacked his sense and control…

Suddenly unease slithered through him, unraveling his surreal state of bliss.

He'd approached her, taken her, as if he was free to make his own choices and pursue his own destiny. And he wasn't.

How had he forgotten that for a minute, let alone a night?

But he *had* forgotten. Totally. And he remembered now.

Dammit, no. It made no difference what was demanded—no, *needed*—of him. There was no way he could blindly point at a bride from the royal catalogue now.

He had no idea how he'd be able to avoid the arranged marriage, but he would. No matter the pressures or the exigencies. Everything in him demanded that he make Gemma his.

He foresaw an epic battle.

He wiped both hands over his face, bunched them in his hair, pulled with a steady, stinging tension as if that would counteract the pressure building inside him.

What a mess.

But what a delight, too.

On the heels of visualizing the upcoming strife, images of her, of them together, conversing, caressing, joined, filled his mind again. In a balance where all the troubles he had piling ahead were weighed against being with Gemma, there was absolutely no contest. Claiming her outweighed the whole world.

He sat up, swung his legs off the bed. He ran his hands over the place where she'd slept—or at least lain—in between their lovemaking sessions. They hadn't slept until morning, too busy talking and experiencing each other in every way, sensual, sexual, mental. His body, already hard, started to pound at him in demand for her.

He tried to convince it to subside. There was no chance it was having her. Not today. After what he'd done to her—twice—no matter how eager she was, she needed at least a couple of days to recuperate.

He got to his feet. "Gemma?"

Silence. He called again, and this time, when the same absence of any sound or movement answered him, the lips that had twitched at imagining her soaking away the aches of his initiation in his tub tightened with alarm. He rushed to the bathroom, burst through the slightly open door.

He almost slumped to the floor at finding it empty. He was in worse shape than he thought. Being with Gemma had just masked his condition. He'd imagined a dozen macabre scenarios during the minute his calls had met with silence.

She had to be in the kitchen. There was no way she could hear him there. Images of her tousled and glowing from a shower, dressed in one of his shirts or lost in one of his bathrobes filled his mind. And she'd be awkward and swollen in all the places that would make him ache until he could barely speak.

He considered walking to her naked, then pulled on pants. She'd let him expose her to every intimacy, had responded with every fiber of her being, but she was still shy when she wasn't in the throes of pleasure. He didn't want to test her more, for now. He'd already rushed her in so many ways. So what if she'd asked him to? That didn't mean he should be so eager to comply. He was the experienced one here, and he shouldn't behave like an overeager teenager.

Seconds after this self-lecture, he was almost running to the kitchen. *Aih,* he *would* embarrass her again.

The premonition hit him before he stepped into the kitchen. All through his penthouse. The feeling of…emptiness. Absence.

The feeling became fact in seconds. The kitchen was also empty.

He didn't stop this time. He whirled around and bolted to inspect each room. Nothing.

Gemma was gone.

He stood in the middle of his living room, overlooking Manhattan, unable to process the knowledge.

She couldn't have just left!

She must have had an overwhelming reason for leaving. Maybe some emergency. Yes. That made sense. But…if something had happened, why hadn't she woken him up? To tell him, to let him help? She knew what kind of power he wielded. If any of her loved ones were in trouble, she knew he'd be the most qualified to help.

Was it possible she didn't realize he'd do anything for her? Was it possible she didn't believe, as he did, that they'd transcended all the conventions of relationship development, had taken a short cut to the highest level one could attain? Or was she so independent that she couldn't bring herself to ask for help because she was determined to deal with whatever problem had cropped up on her own? Or maybe it hadn't occurred to her to ask, in her rush to whatever the emergency was?

Stop. He was probably off base in all of his assumptions, was assigning a ludicrous interpretation to something that would be clear the moment she contacted him.

Something else hit him like a sledgehammer.

He hadn't exchanged any contact info with her.

And it was even worse. He didn't know her last name.

Just what had he been thinking last night?

That was it. He hadn't been thinking. Of anything but her, what they'd shared from first sight onward. He had, for the first time in his life, lived totally in the moment.

He'd always held back from fully trusting others, even his closest people, despite believing in their best intentions. He'd guarded himself against the consequences of their mistakes and misdemeanors. But with Gemma, he hadn't only dropped his guard—it hadn't been raised in the first place. He'd not had a moment of doubt. She was the woman he'd dreamed of but never truly thought he'd find.

The one.

And she was gone. After giving him the most perfect night of his life, after giving him herself and a glimpse of a magnificent future filled with an unprecedented connection, she was just…gone.

Calm down. She'd have an explanation, a perfectly reasonable one, for leaving without waking him up. It had to be the only thing she could have done, or she wouldn't have done it. She wouldn't have left him like that if it weren't.

So he should cool it. He might not know her last name

or her whereabouts, but she knew his. All he had to do was wait for her.

She'd come back the moment she could.

Gemma didn't come back.

It seemed she'd disappeared off the face of the earth.

He'd thought his security detail would have kept tabs on her. But when they'd seen her leave in the early-morning hours, all they'd worried about was him. They'd called to make sure he was okay, and when he'd answered, what he'd remembered doing only when they reminded him, clearly fine but sleepy and brooking no further interruption, they'd let her go. They hadn't seen any reason to follow her. That had destroyed his biggest hope of finding her, and the hope of doing so was becoming dimmer by the minute.

He'd widened his search until it had encompassed the whole United States. No one had heard of her.

With the evidence suggesting that she'd never existed on American soil, he'd begun to think that she and the enchanted night they'd spent together had been a figment of his imagination. Even with his one proof of her existence—the photo he'd taken of her—everyone insisted they'd never seen her. Everyone his people had questioned had commented that they would have remembered someone like her. And they didn't. As for her name, it rang no bells.

It *was* as if she'd never existed.

An explanation had reared its head constantly during his frantic search. He'd knocked it out of the way, determined not to let it have a hearing. But once he'd breathed again with the certainty that she hadn't had an accident or worse, he found his options narrowing down until they'd dwindled to nothing.

Nothing but that explanation made sense.

There was no escaping it anymore. He had to face it, no matter how mutilating it was.

She didn't want to see him again.

She might have been the woman who'd turned his life upside down, but it seemed he'd been nothing to her but a one-night stand. A man she'd chosen to initiate her nubile body into the rites of passion and unlock her limitless sexual potential. Perhaps he'd seemed exotic to her, a man from a different culture and country whom she could cut out of her life once the adventure was over.

Now that resignation had replaced desperation and he'd given up on the dream of her, there was nothing to fight for anymore, nothing to keep him here.

It was time he returned to Zohayd to confront his duty.

To embrace his nightmare.

"Shaheen."

That was all his father said, minutes after Shaheen had walked into his office.

It was enough. Disappointment and exasperation blared in the toneless delivery of his name.

Shaheen didn't blame him. He had ignored his father and the rest of the world for the past eight weeks. After that single phone call telling his father he was not coming home as promised, he'd made himself unavailable to anyone. He hadn't explained why.

His father had left him a dozen messages, had sent emissaries to bring him back or to at least get him to explain his reneging on the decision he'd arrived at only days before.

His father rose from behind his desk, majestic and packed with power and ire and wreathed in the full-blown regalia of the King of Zohayd.

Shaheen held his gaze as his father approached him. King Atef Aal Shalaan made no attempt to hug him as he usually did, but instead stood there, flaying him with his displeasure-radiating glower. His father was a couple of inches shorter, yet broader with more than three decades head start in maturity and responsibility. Shaheen had always thought his shoulders broad enough to carry the weight of the kingdom's fate on them. And that was not to mention his overwhelming presence.

Yet King Atef needed far more than presence to keep the kingdom at peace, to keep his enemies in check and his allies in line. More than ever, he had to appease the most powerful of those who constantly snapped at the heels of the ruling house, demanding their cut of power, prestige and proceeds. And that was something only Shaheen could deliver by sacrificing himself at the literal altar.

His father exhaled, the golden eyes he'd passed down only to Shaheen's brother Harres glittering from below intimidating eyebrows. "I won't ask what made you disappear. Or what brought you back."

"Good." Shaheen didn't attempt to temper his terse mutter. His father would have to be content that he *had* come back. Nothing else was his business.

"But," his father went on, "I'm letting it go only because this is not the time to take you to task over your potentially catastrophic behavior. The reception is in full swing."

The reception. Aka the bridal parade his father had

put together the moment he'd been informed Shaheen was on his way to Zohayd onboard his private jet. He was trapping him into it, before he had a chance to change his mind again.

And there it was, brewing in the main ceremony hall—the storm that would destroy his life. Two thousand people were in attendance, all those with a stake in the marriage and all those involved in the negotiations and manipulations and coercions.

But Shaheen wasn't expected to just flip through the women like he might a mail-order catalog and circle the model he thought most bearable. He was supposed to assess the merchandise in a more comprehensive fashion.

With marriages being what they were in Zohayd—especially the higher you went up the social scale—it was families who married, not individuals. He would have an extended family for a wife. And every potential family was here so that he could decide which one he could best stomach having as a constant presence in his life through their influence on his wife's and children's every thought and action.

"You're not dressed appropriately." His father's reprimand brought him out of his distasteful musings. "I told your *kabeer el yaweran* what was expected of you tonight."

Shaheen's head of entourage *had* said his father wanted him to wear Zohaydan royal garb. He'd scowled at the man and resumed staring blindly at the clauses in his latest business contract.

Now he scowled at his business suit and then at his father with the same leashed aggravation followed by the same pointed dismissal.

His father drew in an equally annoyed breath. "Since

you're flaunting yet another expectation, I demand that you at least wear an expression that doesn't reveal your abhorrence for being here."

Shaheen exhaled in resignation. "Don't ask more of me, Father. A pretense that this isn't torture is foremost among the things I don't have to give."

"You're being unreasonable. You're not the first or last royal to enter a marriage of state for his kingdom's sake."

"And you did it twice, so why not me, eh?" Shaheen knew he was stepping over the line talking to his father, *and* king, this harshly. But he didn't care. He had no more stamina for observing protocol. "And I *am* here to do it, Father. So why should I even attend this farce at all? Why not spare me this added torment? I'd rather not choose the method of my own execution. I'll leave it up to you to pick the most humane one."

King Atef winced at his analogy. "That's the problem. Many candidates have pros and cons that weigh each other out. It has to be your personal preference that tips the balance in one's favor."

"You think I care if I'm shot or electrocuted or cut to pieces? They're all equal and interchangeable to me. Just pick one."

"You're exaggerating now. All your bridal candidates are fine young women. Beautiful, well-bred, highly educated, pleasant. You'll get to like your bride, and maybe in time love her."

"Like you love Queen Sondoss? And loved my mother?"

His father's scowl deepened at Shaheen's ready counter. The best he'd reached with Shaheen's mother was peaceful coexistence. As for Queen Sondoss, leashed hostility was all he could hope for on a good day.

"There are Aliyah and Kamal. I believe no one can be any happier than they are."

"Don't bring them up, Father. They were already crazy in love when they married. Circumstances just forced them apart, and thankfully, forced them back together."

His father's gaze wavered. Then he let go of his kingly veneer.

Nothing remained but the loving father who looked and sounded pained at what he couldn't save his son from. "I can't tell you how much I regret that you'll have to walk in my footsteps. But there's no way around it. And that is why I'm asking you to pay attention to the candidates. At least you have more than one to choose from. I had no say in choosing either your mother or Sondoss. You may have better luck finding someone who's compatible with you among the dozen possible brides."

Shaheen's teeth ground together. He'd already found someone who was compatible with him in every way.

Gemma had clearly not thought the same. She hadn't even thought him worthy of a goodbye.

That didn't change anything for him. He knew now that everything he'd ever dreamed of existed, even if she didn't want him, even if he could never have her. What were the chances that fate would gift him with another woman who was even close?

He not only believed it wouldn't, he didn't want it to.

He refrained from saying anything. His father would have to roll the dice and decide Shaheen's fate himself.

Finally his father gave up, brushed past him and walked out with heavy steps.

Shaheen watched him, compassion flickering through the deadness inside him.

His father hadn't had an easy life. Certainly not a contented one. Shaheen had grown up believing that his father had never known happiness or love outside of what he felt for his job and children. It had been only a couple of years ago that they'd found out he'd once tasted that happiness and love, with a woman. Anna Beaumont.

He'd had an affair with her during his separation from Queen Sondoss two years after Haidar and Jalal were born. Then Anna had fallen pregnant, and his efforts to end his marriage to Sondoss had failed. And though it had nearly destroyed him, he'd left Anna, telling her he could never be with her again, due to the threat of war with Sondoss's home kingdom of Azmahar, and that it was imperative to abort their child.

Instead, Anna had put her baby up for adoption. Shaheen's aunt Bahiyah, secretly knowing about her brother's affair, had adopted Aliyah and passed her off as hers.

It was only many years later, while his father was recovering from a heart attack, that he'd searched for Anna again and discovered the truth. It was a timely discovery, as another flare of unrest in the region could only be resolved if a daughter of King Atef's married the king of Judar. Now Aliyah was King Kamal's worshipped wife and Judar's beloved queen, and Anna Beaumont had become a constant presence in Aliyah's and, by association, his father's lives.

Shaheen believed that had only deepened his father's unhappiness. For he could never have the only woman he'd ever wanted, and as Shaheen sensed, still did.

He and his father had that in common, too.

Shaheen kept his eyes fixed on his father's slumped shoulders as they reached their destination, braced himself as they stepped into the ceremony hall.

Brightness and buzzing seemed to rise at their entry, but he couldn't register the magnificent surroundings beyond the darkness and ugliness inside him. It was reflected on every surface, on every face that turned to look at him.

Suddenly every hair on his body stood on end.

What now?

His eyes panned the room, seeking the source of the disturbance that had drenched him. It now felt as if a laser beam was drilling through his gut.

Then everything came to a grinding halt.

His heart almost ruptured with one startled detonation.

There, at the farthest end of the hall…

Gemma.

Five

Shaheen's mind had snapped. It must have.

He was seeing things.

He swallowed the lump of shock that had lodged into his throat, shuddered as it landed like a brick in his stomach.

He was seeing Gemma.

But he couldn't be. His mind must be projecting the one thing it wanted most, the woman whose memory and taste and touch had been driving him insane and whom he'd despaired of seeing again.

He closed his eyes.

He opened them. She was still there.

"Shaheen, why did you stop?"

He heard his father's concern as if it were coming from a mile away. Gemma, who was at the far end of the two-hundred-foot space, felt mere inches away.

Her gaze snared his across the distance, just like that

first time, was roiling with the same intensity, the same awareness. One thing was missing. Shock.

Of course. She was expecting to see him. There was no element of surprise for her this time. But there was more in her expression. Apprehension. Aversion even.

She was that loath to see him? Then why was she here?

The relevant question hit him harder than the shock of her being here.

How was she here? In Zohayd, in the palace, at this function?

He felt himself moving again, his body activated and steered by his father's hand on his forearm as he led him deeper into the throngs of people gathered to watch his sacrifice.

Moving forced him to relinquish his eye lock with Gemma. He rushed ahead to gain another direct path to her. But she evaded his eyes now, hid from him.

Frustration seethed through him, questions. The urge to cleave through the crowd, push everyone out of the way till he got to her overwhelmed him. He imagined hauling her over his shoulder and storming through the palace to his quarters, pressing her to the nearest upright surface and devouring her.

It wasn't consideration for his father's guests, the most influential people in Zohayd and the region, that stopped him. It was her avoidance. The knowledge that she didn't want him as he wanted her. That whatever had brought her here wasn't him.

For an interminable time, he believed he responded when addressed, monosyllables that he vaguely thought were appropriate, shook hands and grimaced at eager female faces and fawning family members, all the time trying to catch glimpses of her, desperately trying to get her to look at him again.

At one point, his older brother Harres appeared at his side.

"You look out of it, bro. Got stoned to get through this?"

Shaheen felt the urge to deck him. "And what if I did, Mr. Immune-From-This-Abominable-Fate Minister of Interior?"

Harres grimaced. "I did offer to do it myself again. I told them that, unlike you, I don't care one way or another, and I'd certainly remain neutral in my post since I would never get attached to whatever wife they saddled me with. They still refused."

Shaheen's aggression drained. Harres *had* tried to take his place time and again. He would spare him if he could.

He exhaled. "They know you'd get attached to your children."

Harres shrugged. "Maybe. Probably. I don't know. I really can't imagine being a husband let alone a father." He put an arm around Shaheen's shoulder, gave him a hard squeeze of consolation, the golden eyes that could have been their father's flaring with empathy. "I would have done anything to spare you this."

Which Shaheen had just thought. "*Aih,* I know."

He again caught sight of Gemma among the shifting crowd, took an involuntary step nearer as if to force her acknowledgment, resurrect her hunger with his eagerness.

"And *I* know who you're looking at. Who would have thought our little Johara would turn out to be such a stunner?"

Harres's words made no sense. Had Shaheen's mind started to deteriorate from the stress?

Shaheen looked at Harres, *seeing* him for the first time since they'd started talking, the juggernaut knight the kingdom had entrusted with its security, and who'd done the best job in its history. An expression softened his hewn, desert-weathered features, one Shaheen had never seen there except around their female family members. A rare gentleness, a proud indulgence.

And he'd thought Harres had said… No. He couldn't have said that name. Where would it come from, anyway?

He shook his head, desperate to clear it. "What are you talking about?"

"The vision in gold over there. Our Johara…or I should say *your* Johara all grown-up." Harres gave a nod in Gemma's direction. "You've been looking nowhere else since you walked in. And I can't blame you. I gaped at her for a solid ten seconds when Nazaryan greeted me with her on his arm. Who would have thought, eh?"

Shaheen stared at Harres as if he'd started talking in a language he'd never heard before. "Nazaryan?"

Harres snapped his fingers in front of his eyes. "Snap out of it. You're scaring me."

Shaheen shook his head again. "What do you mean Nazaryan?"

"I mean Berj Nazaryan, our royal jeweler, her father."

Shaheen's eyes slid from Harres's, as sluggish and impeded as his thoughts, followed the direction of his earlier nod.

Gemma was the only one in that direction dressed in gold. Harres was talking about her. And he was calling her…calling her…

Johara.

The bubble of incomprehension trembled inside Shaheen. Then it burst.

Gemma was Johara.

Shock mushroomed through him like a nuclear detonation.

His mysterious Gemma was Johara. Berj Nazaryan's daughter. Aram's sister. The girl he'd known since she was six. Who'd become his shadow since the day he'd plucked her out of the air from a thirty-foot fall.

No wonder he'd felt he'd known her forever. *He had.* He *had* recognized her with that first look, even if not consciously.

And no wonder. She looked nothing like the fourteen-year-old she'd been when he'd last seen her. Skinny with glasses and braces, with no ability to wield her femininity the way girls in Zohayd learned to from a very early age. She hadn't only realized her potential, she'd become the total opposite of her former self.

He'd thought he'd seen every brand of beauty this world had to offer. But she was something he'd never thought would be gathered in one woman, all his tastes and fantasies come to life. And that was just on the surface. Deeper, where it counted most, little Johara, as Harres had called her, had become the woman who'd seduced Shaheen on sight, had possessed him in a single night.

He rocked on his feet with the mushrooming realization. Only Harres's hand on his arm steadied him.

Among the storm tossing him about, he managed to answer Harres's worried question. "No, I don't need air. I'm fine."

But he was so far from fine he could be on another planet. He might never be fine again.

He'd taken Johara to his bed.

He'd taken her, in every way, repeatedly.

Just as he thought shock couldn't engulf him any further, his eyes captured her incredible dark ones again. And the final piece of the puzzle crashed down in place. It should have been the first thing he understood the moment he realized who she really was.

He might not have recognized her, but she had known who he was from the first moment. She'd given him enough clues. Her first word to him had been a gasp of his name. She'd later told him all about herself, which had amounted to what he *did* know of her family history, without the names, dates and places.

And when he hadn't clued in, so bowled over by her he hadn't even connected the sun-size dots, she'd chosen to leave him in the dark. The apprehension he felt from her must be her anxiety about his reaction now that she knew he'd finally wised up.

"Now that you've met your potential brides, how is your stomach holding up?"

"Can we give you tips who *not* to choose?"

Shaheen dazedly turned toward the two warm, musical female voices. Aliyah and Laylah flowed to him, hugging him on both sides, reaching up to kiss a cheek each, their exquisite faces brimming with vitality and joie de vivre.

He automatically hugged and kissed them back as the ramifications of what had happened between him and Gemma...*Johara* expanded inside him, squeezing all his vitals.

"The beauty in emerald over there, the one with the incredible black hair down to her feet?" Laylah pinched his cheek playfully as she turned his head in the direction of the woman she was describing, before turning his face back to her quickly. "Don't even look at her again. Her unbelievable locks will turn to serpents at the first opportune moment."

"And the redhead over there." Aliyah directed his gaze toward the woman she was mentioning with more discreet taps on his cheek. "Run if you ever see her again. She grows scales and blowtorches anyone within a mile radius."

Harres laughed. "If you're trying to make Shaheen feel better about this, you're going about it in bizarro fashion."

Laylah poked a teasing elbow into Harres's abdomen. "Hey, we're saving him from settling on the prettiest flower and being devoured alive."

"So now that you've eliminated the most beautiful flowers, do I surmise you think he should go for the ugliest one?"

Aliyah gave a horrified shudder. "Oh, no, *that* one is just as monstrous, without the advantage of being nice to look at. What's inside is on the outside in her case. In fact, we've narrowed down his choices to two."

Harres huffed a sound of pure sarcasm. "Don't tell me. The candidates with the *least* monstrous qualities."

"Actually they're both pretty decent. One is not as accomplished or worldly as Shaheen would prefer, but we believe she would become so as his wife. The other one is really nice, but doesn't have much of a sense of humor. Again, with Shaheen for a husband, she'll definitely develop one."

Shaheen felt as if he'd fallen into the twilight zone, expected to hear a laughter track burst into the background any moment now.

He cleared his throat. "*Shaheen* is right here." The two women squeezed him again, sheepishness coating their expressions. "Thank you, my dears, for vetting my bridal nightmares as only you two discerning ladies could. Write down your choices and hand them to Father. But if he decides one of the monsters is more beneficial to the negotiations, that is who I'll end up with. Anyway, my life as I know and want it is over. So, as I told Father earlier, one catastrophe with which to meet my end is as good as another."

A pall fell on the duo in the wake of his words.

Horror dawned in Aliyah's and Laylah's eyes, contrition twisting their features. They really hadn't realized how much Shaheen hated this, were now mortified that they'd been oblivious to his own distress and teased him about it.

"Oh, Shaheen, I didn't know you were…"

"Oh, Shaheen, I didn't realize…"

Aliyah's and Laylah's apologies stumbled over each other. They fell silent, Aliyah biting her lip, Laylah's eyes filling with tears.

His focus flowed back to its captor, to Gem—to *Johara*. Her eyes darted away the moment his fell on her. She'd been watching him.

A bubble of agitation and elation expanded inside him.

She might be avoiding him, but she *wanted* to look at him and did so the moment she could.

Harres's phone rang.

He answered. After a few terse sentences, he turned his eyes to Shaheen. "I'm sorry to leave you. But something's brewing at our borders. It may take hours or even days to defuse."

Shaheen nodded, accepted Harres's bolstering hug, watched him hug the women and stride away.

Shaheen looked back at the fidgeting Aliyah and

Laylah, a calculating smile spreading his lips even as his heart twisted inside his chest. "How about you atone for your sins by granting this doomed man a last request?"

They both jumped, voices intertwining with promises of anything at all if it would make him feel better.

He looked back at Johara, who again turned her eyes away and bestowed a brittle smile on the group surrounding her.

"Remember Johara Nazaryan?"

Both women looked to Johara.

"Oh, yes," Laylah said. "My mother used to drag me away every time I tried to talk to her. Now look at her, flitting around Johara as if she were an A-list movie star."

Aliyah smirked. "It's not only your mother. All our female relatives and acquaintances who never deemed to speak to her or her mother before are falling over themselves to be reintroduced."

Laylah giggled. "Bless their superficial souls. They never acknowledged what a classy, talented woman Jacqueline Nazaryan was, or what a sweet girl Johara was. But now that Johara has become *the* new designer on the cusp of international stardom, they all want to secure a chance to be the first to wear her latest exclusive designs."

"It's amazing to see that they consider their next outfit more important than their husbands." Aliyah's lips twisted. "Their men are about to flood the ceremony hall in drool, and the women can't care less."

Shaheen blinked, noting the people gathered around Johara for the first time. Women who'd treated her with condescension, or at best the dismissive courtesy due to a valuable employee's family member, were now treating her not just as an equal but as a celebrity.

But it was the men's behavior that made aggression swirl inside him. Many were openly ogling her and courting her attention and favor. His muscles turned to steel as every territorial cell in his body primed for a to-the-death fight for his mate.

Yes. No matter what she'd done or how impossible it all was, his body, his very being, considered her his mate. Accepted nothing else.

Aliyah turned back to him. "What about Johara?"

His burning conviction seemed to force Johara's gaze to him. He muttered, low and hungry, "Bring her to me."

Shaheen was about to combust.

With frustration.

It had been two hours since he'd told Aliyah and Laylah to pluck Johara from her new rabid fans and bring her to him.

After a brief surprise, the two women, who clearly weren't aware of the seriousness of the situation that necessitated his making a marriage of state, thought it a brilliant idea.

They thought he *should* flaunt the royal council's decrees and marry whomever he liked. And with their former connection, who better than Johara?

They'd gone after her as dozens of people inundated Shaheen again. He'd fended them off as he struggled to track the two women's efforts to disentangle Johara from her companions.

After sinking in the quicksand of the court's convoluted maneuvers, the two women could only look on as they lost Johara to another tide of eager fans until she exited the hall.

He had no doubt she'd thwarted them on purpose, had escaped. He had no idea where she'd gone, or if she'd even remain in Zohayd.

By the time he'd freed himself, he'd had a choice between interrogating guards and servants and having the news that he was looking for her spread like wildfire throughout the kingdom, or inspecting every guest suite in the palace himself and causing an even bigger scandal for his—and her—father.

So here he was, pacing his quarters, barely stopping himself from driving his fist through a wall.

He couldn't let her avoid him. He had to confront her. If only for one last time.

Plans were ricocheting in his mind, each seeming more ludicrous than the next, when a knock floated to his ears from his apartment's door.

"Go away," he growled at the top of his voice.

He'd thought whomever was unfortunate enough to seek him now had heeded his order when the knock came again, more urgent.

He stormed to the door, flung it open, ready to blast whomever it was off the face of the earth.

And there she was. Gemma. Johara.

She stood there, in the gold dress that echoed her hair's incredible shades and luster, looking up at him with anxiety in her gaze, a tremor strumming those lush, petal-soft lips he'd been going mad from needing beneath his for eight agonizing weeks.

"Shaheen…"

The memory of that night when she'd said his name, looked at him like that and changed his life forever ripped through him.

He didn't give her a chance to say anything else.

He swooped down on her with the same speed and determination he had two decades ago, when he'd snatched her away from death's snapping jaws. He hauled her into the room, his feet feeling as if they were leaving the ground in his desperation to have her against him, beneath him, *with* him.

Everything merged into a dream sequence. Gemma, Johara, filled his arms, her sweet breath mingling with his, her lips pressing desperately against his own, her flesh cushioning his, her heat and hunger enveloping him.

But questions gnawed at him, eating a hole through his gut as big as the one her disappearance had left in his heart. Why had she withheld the truth from him, why had she left him that way, why had she chosen now to come back, and the most important question of all—had she come back for him?

Nothing came out but an agonized, *"How could you?"*

She jerked as if the words singed her. She wrenched away, pressed her face into the bed. "You're angry."

"Angry?" He rose on one elbow, gazed down at her trembling profile. "You think I'm *angry?*"

"N-no." The tears he could see glittering in her eyes welled, spilled over to drench her cheek, making a wet track down to lips that trembled. "You're way more than angry. You're enraged. And outraged. And y-you have every right to be both."

"I'm none of those things. I'm…I'm…" He sat up, raked his hands through his hair, felt close to tearing it out. "I still can't believe you did this to me."

"I'm so sorry. I know I should have told you who I was…"

"Yes, you should have. But that isn't what I meant. How could you leave me like that? Didn't you realize how I'd feel? I felt…" He paused as she hesitantly turned to face him, searched for the words to describe his desperation and desolation after her disappearance. Nothing came to him but one word. It gashed out of him *"Bereaved."*

She lurched as if he'd shot her. Emotion crumpled her face, and more tears poured from her.

He studied her, paralyzed by the enormity of the distress radiating from her, then he reached for her, even now fearing he'd grab thin air. He groaned his remembered anguish as he pressed her harder into him, lost the ability to breathe as her precious body filled his empty arms, when he'd despaired he'd ever hold her this close again.

"I never intended for any of that to happen." She sobbed on his shoulder. "I-I only came to the party to see you, didn't dream you wouldn't recognize me. But when you didn't…when you were…"

He pulled back to watch her, to fill his eyes with the reality of her, her nearness, threaded his aching fingers into her hair. "Were what? All over you? Out of my mind with wanting you on sight?"

"I never imagined things could go that far. I thought I'd see you one last time before you got married and I no longer had the right to…to… I should have told you who I am, but I knew if I did, you would pull back, treat me like an old acquaintance, and I couldn't give up that time with you. If I'd told you, you certainly wouldn't have made love to me. So I didn't, and I-I compromised you. And I had to leave before I did anything even worse."

Shaheen stared down at her, life flooding back into him.

This was why she'd left. She'd thought she had to. For his sake. It had been as magical for her as it had been for him. She wanted him as much as he wanted her, and it had killed her as much as it had him when she'd walked away.

But one thing stopped his elation in its tracks. Her mortification, her self-blame. Setting her straight took precedence over every other consideration.

He grabbed her hands, covered them in kisses. "You're wrong, my Gemma, *ya joharti,* my Johara. You didn't compromise me—you energized me, stabilized me. You liberated and elated me. And you were wrong about your doubts, too. I might have hesitated when I found out who you were, mostly from surprise, but *nothing* would have stopped me from taking you. Nothing but you, if you didn't want me."

Her tears stopped abruptly, the remorse dimming her eyes then giving way to the fragility of disbelief, relief and finally the radiance of wonder.

His heart expanded, his world righting itself. A hand behind her head and another behind her back gathered her to him, fitting her into him, the half he'd felt had been torn away from his flesh.

"But you wanted me," he murmured into her mouth, tasting her, plucking at her clinging lips, over and over. "You still want me."

She moaned, opened to him, let him into her recesses, the most potent admission of desire. He took it all, gave more, one thing filling his awareness. His Johara was back in his arms. And he planned to keep her there, to never let her go again.

He told her. "And I'll never stop wanting you."

* * *

Johara cried out as Shaheen's lips came down on hers in full possession. Her world spun in a kaleidoscope of delight, her body in a maelstrom of sensation.

But she wasn't here for this.

No matter that she'd been dying for him, shriveling up from deprivation.

She dug her shaking fingers into the vital waves of his hair, tried to tug at them, to have him allow her a breath that didn't pass through both their bodies. Before he dragged her any deeper into pleasure, submerged her into union with him. She failed.

But as if sensing her struggle, he withdrew his lips from hers lingeringly, rose to look down at her, his eyes a mixture of tenderness and ferocious possession. "What is it, *ya joharti?* Your heart is flapping so hard I can feel it inside my own chest."

"Th-this isn't why I came here, Shaheen. I just wanted to explain, to say goodbye—"

"There will be no goodbyes between us, *ya galbi.* Never."

Before she could cry out that there would be, no matter what either of them wanted, he claimed her lips again.

And she drowned. In him, in her need, in a realm where only he existed and mattered. She let herself sink, promising herself it would be the last time…

"I'm sorry. I did knock. Repeatedly."

Johara jerked as the soft apology came from far, far away, shattering the cocoon enveloping her and Shaheen. She shuddered, felt Shaheen stiffen above her.

"Get out of here, Aliyah."

Silence met his growl, then a distressed intake of breath.

"I'm really sorry, Shaheen, but this can't wait."

Johara lurched again as Aliyah's strained words brought the outside world crashing back on her like an avalanche.

Earlier, Aliyah and Laylah had tried to cajole her into speaking with Shaheen. She'd made her escape then, thinking she'd saved him from making more compromising mistakes because of her. But if she'd feared any suspicion of their relationship would tarnish his image and hurt his marriage plans, she'd done far worse now. She'd just given Aliyah evidence.

She lay beneath Shaheen, her dress riding up to her waist, her splayed legs accommodating his bulk as his hands cupped her buttocks through her panties and his hardness ground against her. Her dress hung off one shoulder exposing half a breast that had just been engulfed in his mouth.

Mortification drenched her, all the more so because the arousal coursing through her didn't even slow down. She wouldn't have been able to bolt out of the room even if she wasn't pinned down by Shaheen. She couldn't move.

She didn't need to. Shaheen relinquished his possession of her flesh with utmost tranquility, rearranged her clothes with supreme care. Then he scooped her up from the bed and steadied her on her feet, smoothing her mussed hair, gently massaging her worried features.

With one last look of reassurance, one last, lingering kiss, he turned to his sister.

Aliyah looked an apology at Johara. It was clear she did have a paramount reason for being there. One she wasn't about to divulge in Johara's presence.

Seeing this unfortunate development as an opportunity to escape, Johara rushed forward to leave.

Shaheen's hand on her arm stopped her.

"Please, Shaheen," she choked out, hoping that Aliyah, who'd moved away discreetly, wouldn't hear. "Let me go. I'll soon be gone and you won't see me again, for real this time. I beg you, for as long as I must stay in Zohayd, you must stay away from me."

She bolted away, gathering the heavy layers of her silk dress in her hands so her stumbling legs wouldn't snarl in their folds.

She still almost fell on her face when she heard his beloved voice behind her, intense, low, permeated with voracity and finality.

"There is no way I will stay away from you, *ya joharti*."

Six

"This had better be good, Aliyah."

Shaheen heard irritation sharpening his voice as he closed the door. He stood there, vibrating with the need to storm after Johara. Instead, he turned to Aliyah. He'd never been upset with her in his life, but he was furious with her now. Not because she'd interrupted his and Johara's surrender to their deepening bond, or because he was seething with frustration. But because her intrusion had upset Johara, had given her another reason to pull back from him.

Johara evidently knew about the gravity of his situation, as often the families of those who worked in sensitive areas in the palace did. And she had extreme feelings about compromising him. She'd put them both through hell so she wouldn't. She must think Aliyah witnessing their lovemaking the ultimate exposure.

And instead of only fighting the world for her, he

now had to fight against her own anxieties, too. He had to convince her to stop trying to do what she thought was right for him, to let him worry about his problems, to realize his best interests lay in having her with him.

He still had no idea how he'd achieve that, but now that he knew she'd never really left him, still wanted him, he would renege on his promise to his father, to his kingdom. He would face anything on earth to be with her, come what may.

"Actually this is bad. As bad as can be," Aliyah finally answered his exasperation, her voice measured.

And in spite of the situation and what she'd just said, his heart softened with love and admiration for her.

Aliyah had had the harshest life of them all, had triumphed over impossible odds. He still couldn't believe how she'd come back from a prescription drug addiction that doctors' misdiagnoses and overanxious parents had plunged her into, how she'd made the decision to face her addiction and the world alone at the tender age of sixteen. It never ceased to be a pleasure for him to see her so healthy, to watch her blossoming daily with Kamal's love, settling deeper in contentment with the blessing of their happiness and two children and filling her position as one of the most beloved queens in the world.

He watched her as she approached with the grace of the old supermodel and the new queen. She was truly regal, dressed in honeyed-chocolate, the color of her eyes; she was as tall as Johara, if differently proportioned. But her every step closer struck a chord of foreboding in his heart.

She stopped before him, her turmoil more obvious close up. She gestured to herself. "See anything wrong with this picture?"

"Is this about you?" He took her by the shoulders, his eyes feverishly scanning her. "Are you…" He stopped, swallowed the ball of panic that suddenly blocked his throat. "Are you okay?"

She reached out an urgent hand to his face. "Oh, I'm fine. It's not about me. It's about these."

His gaze followed her hand to where it rested on the magnificent diamond-and-precious-stone necklace gracing her swanlike neck. Matching earrings dangled to her shoulders and an elaborate web-ring bracelet adorned her wrist.

"What about them?" he asked, mystified. "Apart from looking more incredible with your beauty showcasing them?"

"Father did give them to me to showcase for this function. They are part of the Pride of Zohayd." Shaheen nodded. He recognized them as part of the royal jewels, Zohayd's foremost national treasure. "I was supposed to return them as soon as I took them off, as you know, but as I did I…"

"What? You…damaged them?"

If she had, Berj Nazaryan would fix them, and no one should be the wiser. Because if anyone found out, the situation *would* be grave.

Her gaze grew darker. "No. I discovered they're fake."

He gaped at her.

Fake. *Fake*.

The word revolved in his mind, gaining momentum, until it catapulted him forward to touch the jewels, to inspect them.

He raised confused eyes to her. "They look the same."

"That's the whole idea of good fakes. And these are nothing short of *incredible*."

Logic tried to make a stand. "But you're not a jewelry expert. And you probably haven't worn those before."

"I did far more than wear them. You remember I was almost catatonic when I was in my early teens? Well, my shrinks recommended I have a creative outlet as part of my 'therapy.' I wanted to paint, and the only thing I wanted to paint was the jewels. Mother Bahiyah got me into the vaults regularly to paint them."

So she did know the jewels intimately.

Denial took over from logic. "But it's been so many years since you saw them."

"Time doesn't make any difference with my photographic memory. Tiny discrepancies screamed at me from the moment I took a good look at them. But without comparing them to detailed photos of the originals, I'm sure no one else would notice. No one but the experts, that is."

Shaheen felt the frost of dread spread through him. He'd seen evidence of her infallible memory. As a supremely talented professional artist, Aliyah used it now to produce paintings with uncanny detail.

If she thought the jewels were fakes, they were.

His shoulders slumped under the enormity of the conviction.

Aliyah joined him in the deflation of defeat, lowered her eyes, then exhaled and tucked a mahogany tress behind her ear. She lifted her gaze back to his. "My first instinct was to rush to Harres with this. I did try to call him, but he's incommunicado. I then thought of Amjad as our eldest, but I realized it should be you I told first. For now."

He blinked, nothing making sense anymore. "What do you mean?"

"My decision was based on your past connection

to Johara and the special interest you showed in her tonight. But then I came here and discovered it was far more than special interest. This isn't the first time this happened between you. I could tell. Your passion, the depth of your involvement, almost burned me from twenty feet away. You're her lover, aren't you?"

"You..." Shaheen shook his head, still trying to assimilate her revelations. And assumptions. "You think Johara has something to do with this?"

Aliyah let her shoulders drop. "I honestly don't know what to think. Between father and daughter, Berj and Johara are not only among the few who have access to the jewels, they're among the few in the *world* capable of faking them. And then, there is her sudden reappearance in Zohayd and in the palace."

Shaheen's numbness evaporated under the ferocity of the need to defend Johara. "She came back for *me*."

Aliyah's gaze grew wary. "Is this what she told you?" He looked at her helplessly, because Johara hadn't said that. Aliyah went on, her voice more subdued. "She came back three weeks ago. I was here visiting mother Bahiyah the day after her arrival. And I met her. She said she came back to see her father. The father who resigned his post as royal jeweler just before the reception."

This time when she fell silent, Shaheen felt he'd never be able to talk ever again.

When the silence grew too suffocating, she sighed. "I can't believe either of them could do something like this, either. But then, who knows what's been going on with Berj? Mother Bahiyah told me tonight she wasn't surprised when he quit, said he hasn't been himself for a while. She said he'd been getting more morose, withdrawn, empty-eyed. And then he had a heart attack."

The new shock forced his voice to work. "*Ya Ullah,* when?"

"Three months ago."

"Why did no one tell me?" Berj, the endlessly kind and patient, stunningly creative man, like his son and daughter, had always been one of the dearest people to Shaheen. He loved him more than he loved any of his uncles.

"According to mother Bahiyah, he made Father promise not to tell anyone, even his family," she assured him. Then she reluctantly added, "But maybe he felt his mortality, knew he wouldn't be able to work for much longer. Maybe our enemies got to him."

"To offer him what? Financial security? Do you think Father didn't reward his two-decade career with our family more generously than anything anyone else could offer? Though the job has never been about money for Berj, he can now live a retired life of leisure and luxury. And if he doesn't want that, he can afford to start his own business. He doesn't even have any dependents to worry about. All his family are financially independent in their own right."

"He might have a problem that depleted his funds—gambling, for instance." Aliyah shrugged. "I'm as confused as you are. I'm just pointing out that he hasn't been himself. And then, Johara has changed beyond all recognition, on the surface. What if she's changed on the inside, too, and—"

He growled his unconditional belief in Johara, cutting Aliyah off. "*No.* No, she hasn't. She's still our Johara. *My* Johara."

Aliyah looked at him with the same caution she would look at an enraged tiger who might lash out at any second. "I never really knew her, but I always got good vibes from her. I only met her again that day three weeks ago, then again tonight. I did like her again on sight, much more now that we're both grown-up. But though I don't see her as a manipulator, I do get the feeling she's hiding something. Something big."

"It's her relationship with me."

"No. I felt it again just now, when there was…nothing to hide about *that* anymore."

He glowered down at her. "You won't make me doubt her."

"I'm just presenting you with the facts. I'd hate to think anything bad, let alone something that bad, of Berj and Johara, but right now I'm at a loss to come up with another explanation."

"There *is* another explanation. Everything you mentioned is circumstantial evidence. Nothing more."

"True. But we can't afford to overlook any possibilities. This is too huge, Shaheen. The fate of the royal house—the whole kingdom—depends on it."

Silence crashed again.

At last, Aliyah drew in a ragged breath. "What shall we do?"

"*You* will hand back the jewels as if you didn't notice anything. And you will *not* say anything to anyone. Starting with Amjad and Harres. Give me a few days to sort this out."

"Are you sure, Shaheen?"

There were no hesitation in him. "Yes."

Aliyah chewed her lip, worry etched on her face. "I did want to give you a chance to sort this out. But that was before I walked in on you and Johara. You're in love with her, aren't you?" Shaheen only nodded. He was. Irrevocably. She exhaled. "Are you sure you can handle this? Do you think you can be objective?"

He wouldn't even dignify that with an answer. "Give me your word that you'll let me handle this, will let me recruit Harres and Amjad into the matter at my discretion."

"You're going to search for proof Johara and Berj have nothing to do with it, aren't you? What if you don't find any? What if we don't have the time for you to investigate?"

"We have time."

"How do you know that?"

"Think about it, Aliyah. The forgers probably faked all of the Pride of Zohayd collection, or they would have somehow made sure you were handed authentic pieces to wear tonight. But since no claim has been leaked that we failed to protect the jewels from theft, the thieves and forgers are waiting for the time when the biggest scandal can be achieved."

Horror dawned on Aliyah's face. "The Exhibition Ceremony!"

He nodded grimly. "Yes. And that's still months away. So we have time. And I *will* take every possible second of it. Give me your word that you'll let me have it, Aliyah."

Aliyah's expression filled with conflict as she met his gaze head-on. He struggled to bring his emotions under control so he wouldn't give her more cause to doubt his judgment.

She finally nodded. "You have it. And Kamal's, too."

"You told him!"

"I tell him everything." She suddenly dragged him into a fierce hug. "If you love her like I love Kamal, I wish nothing more than for you to prove her innocence, that you can have her and love her."

He hugged her back for a long moment. Then he kissed the top of her head. She looked up at him one last time then walked out.

Shaheen staggered to the nearest chair, sank down onto it.

It was all too much to take in.

The bridal ordeal, finding Johara here, what happened since. Now Aliyah's discoveries. Their possible explanations and ramifications. Yet one thing trumped it all.

Johara wasn't here for him. She was here for her father.

Yet the realization didn't pain him. She thought she had no place in his life. She hadn't thought she *could* come back for him. In fact, it must have been torture for her to attend the reception tonight. To not only know he was getting married to someone else, but to watch him pick that wife.

And Berj had chosen tonight of all nights to hand in his resignation, and hours later, Aliyah discovered that his paramount duty, safeguarding the jewels, had been compromised.

No. He couldn't doubt him. And he would never doubt Johara. There *was* another explanation.

But until he found it, this was a catastrophe in the making.

The Pride of Zohayd jewels were far more than the foremost national treasure.

Legend had it that each piece of jewelry opened doors where none existed, attained coveted results where they had seemed impossible, courted monarchs' favor, brought true love, achieved undying glory and even cheated death.

Five hundred years ago, when tribal wars in the territories that had yet to become Zohayd were at their peak, Ezzat ben Qassem Aal Shalaan knew that on the day the leadership of his tribe fell to him, he'd need more than wisdom, power and military triumphs to bring an end to the conflicts and gather the tribes under his rule.

He'd followed the history of each jewel, charted an infallible plan to possess them all and wield unparalleled authority. To his father's horror, he left the tribe when he was only eighteen and went on his quest to collect those jewels from all over the Asian continent.

It took him twelve years to do it, but on his return, the tide turned in his tribe's favor, and within months, he'd united the tribes and became the first king of Zohayd. Together, he and the jewels had become known as the Pride of Zohayd.

The jewels became the symbol of the royal family's entitlement to the throne. Legend went on to say that they remained in no one's hands if unworthy of the privilege and power.

Each year for the past five centuries, Aal Shalaan monarchs had held a week of festivities to renew their claim to the throne, culminating in a grand ceremony to exhibit the jewels to representatives of the Zohaydan people as proof that the Aal Shalaans remained the rightful rulers of the land.

There was only one reason the jewels would be stolen and replaced by fakes.

This was an insidious plot to overthrow the ruling family.

For what felt like hours, his mind raged with scenarios and solutions. Each time one started to seem possible, he slammed into a dead end.

He felt he'd been battered by the time he got to his

feet, a basic plan—the only one he believed could work—in mind.

To set it in motion, he had to get away from the palace.

And get Johara out, too.

She had to get out of here.

That was the only thing on Johara's mind since she'd stumbled away from Shaheen.

All through the palace to her quarters, she'd struggled to walk naturally and greet the workers who were everywhere in the aftermath of the reception, undoing its havoc.

By the time she reached her room, she couldn't remain upright, slumped against the door to stop herself from collapsing to the ground.

Her body was still in turmoil, her whole being rioting. She wanted to run back to Shaheen's quarters and throw herself in his arms. Come what may.

But she couldn't. Ever again.

And not only would she be deprived of him forever, she'd probably be here to witness his marriage, if her father still needed her by the time it came to pass.

"I did it."

Johara's heart almost burst through her ribs. She swung around, found her father walking in from her suite's kitchenette. He looked as if he'd aged another ten years.

"I handed in my resignation to the king."

So he'd finally done it! He'd attended the reception with her, stood beside her for most of it, and hadn't said a word. He hadn't said a word, period. He was taking this even harder than she'd thought.

The desolation in his voice sent compassion surging

through her, propelling her to him so she could hug him, absorb his misery.

He let out a ragged breath, accepted her silent embrace.

Then he pulled back with a sad smile, love shining in the eyes he'd passed down to her. "You always know what to do and say. And more important, what *not* to do and say. I don't think I could have stomached platitudes about how it's for the best, how it's time to start a new life."

A smile trembled on her face in an attempt at teasing. "Even though it's true."

He pinched her cheek softly. "Especially since it is."

She smiled back into his eyes, thankful that he was letting her steer him away from moroseness.

She'd been urging him to resign for the past three weeks, since the day she'd come back and he'd told her he was thinking it was the solution to everything, to sever his connection to Zohayd. And he'd had no idea of *her* dilemma.

She couldn't have agreed more. Yet it had taken him this long to bring himself to do it.

"This place, these people, are far more than a job to me." He walked to the nearest couch, sat down with a heavy exhalation.

She nodded. "Mother always said they held your heart as much as we did, but with the added feeling that you were doing something far bigger than yourself, playing a major part in maintaining the peace and prosperity of Zohayd."

"It's not a feeling, it's a fact." A faraway look of bittersweet reminiscence came over his face. "She once told me I was delusional, considering myself a knight who swore undying allegiance to a great king. But it's not a delusion. I am, and he is." He looked back at her, dejection dimming his gaze. "The only reason I'm ending my service is because I'm no longer in any shape to deliver what he deserves. Even as I lost my family, first Jacqueline, then you, then Aram, I still… functioned. But lately, I seem to have lost my focus, my skills, my stamina."

"You never lost *us*. We love you!"

"But you're no longer with me. Did you know I've been begging your mother to come back to me and to convince you to return, too?"

No. That was news to her. Her parents' relationship had always been a mystery.

"My efforts intensified after Aram went back to the States six years ago. She always refused, so I came to see you both more, stayed longer each time. When he realized my need to be with you, King Atef went out of his way to afford me extended leaves."

She'd wondered how he'd been able to visit them for such long periods. Each visit had always left Jacqueline Nazaryan distraught.

"Your mother has never stopped loving me, you know?"

Johara looked at him helplessly. It seemed he had suddenly decided to answer all the questions he and her mother had always evaded. It had always been impossible to fathom her mother when it came to her father. Jacqueline talked about him and to him with such ire and intensity, but she'd never asked for divorce, or hooked up with another man.

Now Johara watched her father smile to himself, the smile of a man remembering the woman he loved, a sensual pain filling his eyes and lips. "We're still lovers."

She inhaled. Now that was something they'd both left her in the dark about. Very efficiently. She doubted she and Shaheen could hide the intimate nature of their relationship that well. Or at all. Which was why she must never be seen with him again.

She exhaled. "Why won't she come back?"

That would have saved *her* from coming back herself and seeing Shaheen again, driving the lance in her heart deeper.

Her father's lips twisted. "Because she's angry at me. She's been angry at me for a decade and a half. There was a time when I thought she might come back, but then you joined her and she's been adamant ever since about not returning to Zohayd, even for a visit."

"That's why you didn't tell her about your heart attack. Or your depression."

His nod was defeated. "I won't pressure her by playing on her sympathy, Johara. And I certainly don't want her pitying me. I chose my duty over her. I've made a mess of things, and that won't be how I win her back. But I intend to. Or die trying, anyway."

She gasped and he made an apologetic wave of his hand as he rose from the couch. "Don't listen to me, I'm feeling sorry for myself. I'll snap out of it. All the faster because you're here. I've never felt this fragile, and I think my condition makes me more prone to clinging to what I have here. It was your presence that gave me the strength to do what I did tonight. Will you please stay until I serve my notice?"

Her father had never asked anything of her until he'd asked her to come be by his side through this.

She couldn't say no then. She couldn't say it now. She nodded, surged to hug him again.

As she watched him walking out of her suite, her heart churned out thick, slow thuds.

She was trapped. She'd survived being in Zohayd with Shaheen out of the kingdom, but now…

Even after the night of magic they'd shared, she hadn't really believed he might react that way when he saw her again. During the past eight weeks, she'd tormented herself that, with his impending marriage in motion, when they met, he'd pretend she was the acquaintance he hadn't seen in years and then ignore her.

But he hadn't. He'd been every bit as incredible as he'd been that night. She had the same effect on him that he had on her, making him forget caution and trample on reason.

She couldn't let him do that.

Until she could escape Zohayd, this time forever, she had to do everything she could to stop him from destroying his and his family's credibility and weakening their power.

Most of all, she had to keep her secret intact.

A secret that, if discovered, might cost the Aal Shalaans their throne.

Seven

After coming to his decision, Shaheen had ambushed his father as he'd prepared to sleep.

He'd told King Atef he'd changed his mind. He was relieving him of the burden of choosing his bride. But he wanted more choices. Or more reason to choose one of the existing candidates over the others. Surely the families didn't think a prettier dress or a more practiced smile would sway him? Didn't they have more… incentives? For him, personally? He was not just the king's son, a body with the required genes. He was a force to be reckoned with throughout the world. It was his life they were bartering away, after all, and they'd better make it worth his while.

His father had only closed his eyes then risen from his bed and walked out of his room without looking at Shaheen.

Shaheen shut his own eyes now. He hated to add to

his father's strife. But he couldn't include him in his plan. Not yet.

His plan was simple. Kick up a controversy, drag in all those involved in his dilemma and stand back and watch. People showed their true colors in conflicts.

And that was what had been missing so far. After they'd agreed that Shaheen would pick a family through its representative bride, the tribes had fallen into a peaceful coexistence, thinking that, with Shaheen's reputation for being completely incorruptible, there was nothing they could do beyond parading their daughters before him to influence his decision.

Now he'd as good as told them he wasn't just acting the king's obedient son in this matter and they should indeed fight dirty for said favor.

The reactions to this new development—and most important, the nonreactions—would expose who among their so-called allies who had access inside the palace were after new treaties within the current ruling regimen, and who was planning a coup.

He'd thrown his bomb and retreated, gone to his villa on the waters of the Arabian Sea, a hundred miles from the palace. He'd be inaccessible yet still be able to monitor the developments as the reactions of those involved reached him one way or another. Most important, he'd see Johara away from the scrutiny of the court.

She was coming to him now.

His heart expanded at the thought of her. It had taken every iota of his negotiating skills to secure her agreement. And she'd amazed him all over again.

She hadn't resisted because she was feeling jealous or slighted or even heartbroken that he was seeking her out even as he went ahead with his marriage plans.

She'd done so because she didn't want to stir up trouble for him.

But though making everyone believe he was still in the game was paramount for his plan's success, none of that mattered. Not when weighed against protecting her from hurt.

He couldn't leave her in the dark about his feelings and about what he had planned.

She'd agreed to come only when he'd told her he'd come to her publicly if she didn't. She'd believed he was desperate enough to do it. But she'd insisted on making her own way. She'd said no one would think anything of her driving away from the palace on her own, but if she left in his chauffeured car, it would probably be on the national news within the hour. She'd even asked him to send his entourage away while she visited him. Since there was nothing he wanted more than to be alone with her, he'd emptied the immediate two-mile radius.

He was now standing on his second-floor bedroom suite's veranda, awaiting her arrival. He cast his impatience across the tranquil emerald waters, followed the curve of the bay that hugged them and the villa, untouched by human hands except for the road that arced along its edge and that would bring her to him.

The sea winked diamonds in the pre-sunset rays as it lapped froth on the white-gold shore, its mass rocking gently back and forth, its rumble a hypnotic loop. The dense palm trees embracing the villa on its eastern and northern sides swayed in the strong autumn breeze in a dance of rustling elegance and harmony.

The magnificence and serenity felt lifeless, lacking. When she arrived everything would come alive, would be complete.

A cloud of dust swirled at the edge of his vision. In moments it parted on a streak of silver. A speeding car.

"Johara."

He whispered her name, again and again, as he ran through the villa and grounds to await her at the gates.

In minutes, she pulled the car to a gentle stop, feet from him. He covered the remaining distance, holding her eyes through the windshield. He ended up leaning down to plant his palms flat on the hood of her father's Mercedes, trying to bring the longing under control. Then he saw her mouth his name, the feelings echoing his trembling over her face. And he failed.

He rushed to her side, yanked her door open. Then she was in his arms, and he was in hers.

He took her from gravity as he wished to from everything that caused her worry. She surrendered herself to his haven, arms enveloping him from neck to back. He savored their connection, letting their eyes embrace, mate, love welling through him as he pressed her closer and closer. Then he took her lips.

She whimpered his name and he groaned hers between kisses so urgent they grew from barely letting their flesh connect, to sealing their lips in wrenching fusions.

They only broke apart when he placed her on his bed.

He loomed above her, looking down into her eyes, waiting for her to show him, to ask him.

She did, in every way. Her swollen lips joined her misty eyes in their demands, trembled on his name, begging for him.

He'd promised himself he'd talk to her first. But while he could have denied his own craving, he couldn't deny hers.

He rose and her arms fell off his body. They thudded on the dark brown silk he'd draped his bed with for her, graceful arcs of surrender surrounding her head and fanned golden hair. Then she arched upward sinuously, in a wave of white-hot desire stroking him from thighs to chest.

He shuddered with the effort not to tear her out of her clothes and ram into her. His hands trembled when he forced gentleness into them as he stripped her out of her beige pantsuit, which could have been the most outrageous lingerie for its effect on him. He descended deeper into mindlessness as her twists and undulations helped him expose her lushness for his voracity.

"You have no idea, my Gemma..." He kissed and suckled his way from her feet, up her endless satin legs, turning her on her stomach to devour the firmness of her thighs and buttocks, to dig massaging fingers and mouth into the grace of her back and neck. "No idea, what I went through, when you disappeared. Worry almost destroyed my sanity. Then misery, when I thought you didn't want me."

"No." Her cry tore through him as he ground himself against her back, finesse and restraint evaporating. Moans filled his head, high and deep, hers and his. Her flesh burned him with its own torment as she struggled beneath him, demanding he let her face him. He did, and she sank her fingers in his hair, tugged, her eyes urgent, adamant, solemn. "I've never wanted anything but you, Shaheen."

"And I never knew what wanting was until you." Her tears spilled at his declaration. He kissed them away, put her hands to his shirt. "Show me how much you want me, *ya galbi.*"

The hunger that spread over her face made him unable to bear the speed with which she exposed him. He ripped anything that couldn't be undone fast enough, hoping she wouldn't be alarmed at his savagery. Relief flooded him when it only inflamed her more.

But it wasn't every dig of her fingers, nip of her teeth, pull of her lips, or even that she overcame her shyness and stroked and tasted his manhood that made him almost berserk. It was her words that singed him through to his soul and served as the ultimate aphrodisiac.

"I always thought you the most beautiful thing in the world, Shaheen," she sobbed. "I want you all over me, inside me."

"Give me your pleasure first, *ya galbi.*"

Before she could protest, he clamped one nipple between his lips, suckled her, nipped her, gorging on the feel and taste. Her cries of pleasure amplified in his inflamed brain as her body begged for his invasion. He glided the length of his nakedness against hers, reveling in how her satin firmness cushioned his rougher hardness. He pushed her legs apart with his knees, opened her folds with one hand. He stumbled to the brink just gliding his fingers along her molten heat, just smelling her arousal.

He drew harder on her nipple, giving her two fingers to suckle, while his other hand rubbed shaking circles over the knot of flesh where her nerves converged. She writhed, moaned, rippled beneath him, demanding more. He gave her more, two fingers pumping into her tight, flowing heat. After a few languorous thrusts, she bowed up on a stifled cry. Then she came apart.

"*Aih, ya galbi,* show me how much you want everything I do to you." He feasted on the sight as she took her fill of pleasure, her inhibitions almost gone. Each grip and release of her inner flesh on his fingers transmitted to his arousal.

He still waited until she subsided, then stimulated her again. She pushed his hand away with a sharp cry of impatience, snared him with her legs, trying to get him to mount her.

He smiled his approval into her stormy eyes. "*Aih,* show me what you want of me, tell me how you want it."

"I want you to take me, hard. Don't you dare hold anything back this time. Give me all of you—" her fingers dug into his shoulders, wrenching him down on top of her with all the power of her fervor "*—now!*"

Before he complied, he reached for the bedside drawer. He was ready with protection this time. She stayed his hand, shook her head. Holding her heavy-with-need gaze, he read her message. She was telling him it was safe to take her. And he couldn't draw another breath if he didn't, if he didn't give her all of him. He gripped her buttocks, tilted her, growled, "*Khodini kolli*...take all of me, *ya joharti,*" and plunged.

He hit her womb on that first thrust, obeying her need for his total invasion, secure she was ready, that any discomfort would only sharpen her pleasure. She engulfed him back with a piercing keen, consumed him in what felt like a velvet inferno.

He rested his forehead on hers, feeling like he was truly home, his hold on consciousness loosening.

Then she arched beneath him, until he felt she took him into her core, her streaming eyes making him feel she'd taken him into her heart. She was embedded in his.

With a pledge that he'd never let her go, he withdrew all the way then thrust back, fierce and full.

He rode every satin scream as hard as she'd demanded, his rumbling echoing her cries. Her tightness clamped harder around his length, pouring more red-hot pleasure over his flesh, until she convulsed beneath him.

Seeing her abandon, feeling the force of her pleasure, shattered him. He plummeted after her into the abyss of ecstasy, slid himself all the way inside her and released his essence.

Time ceased to matter, to exist, as he came down on top of her as she demanded, anchoring her after the tumult.

Then he brought her over him, a drape of satisfaction, everything he wanted wanting him back, and back in his arms.

"Ahebbek, ya joharti. Aashagek. Enti hayati kollaha."

She jerked at the words he whispered against her cooling forehead. Then she pushed feebly against him, demanding to be released from their union.

It took a moment before he could bring himself to release her, worry replacing satiation and bliss at her agitated breathing and renewed tears, which he was sure didn't indicate renewed arousal.

"Don't…say things like that again." She wiped tears away, half stricken, half furious. "I believe you want me like you've never wanted another, but don't say what you can't possibly feel."

He sat up, caught her face in both hands, made her look at him. "That *is* how I feel. And more."

Thicker tears overflowed from her reddened eyes. "How can you? How can you love me, worship me, think that I'm all your life? Before today, we had only one night together."

"We had eight *years*. And all the years we've been apart. I loved you each moment of those." A sob tore through her as she shook her head, tried to escape his grip again. He wouldn't release her, persisted. "Why do you find it unbelievable? *You* loved me each moment of those years."

She dipped her head, her hair swishing forward in waves that looked like sun rays spun into glossy satin, obscuring her expression. "I…never said I loved you."

"Yes, because you're trying not to 'compromise' me, or 'impose' on me, by keeping this on the level of the senses, and away from the domains of the heart and soul."

She bit her trembling lower lip. "W-why do you think that?"

"Because I know you. I've known everything about you since you were six and grew up under my proud eyes. You didn't just share everything you thought with me, you shared *how* you thought. I can predict everything that goes inside your brilliant if misguided mind and your magnanimous, self-sacrificing heart. That's why I love you so completely. And you love me as totally, as fiercely. I feel it. I felt it from the first moment I met you again. I might not have recognized you consciously, but everything in me knew you, and knew I had always loved you."

She gaped at him. And gaped at him. Then she burst in tears.

"Oh, Shaheen…I n-never dreamed you c-could feel the same." Words tore from her between sobs. "If I'd known, I wouldn't have tried to see you again. I don't want to complicate your life."

He pressed her hard, stopping her self-blame again.

"As I told you last night, you've done nothing but make my life worthwhile. In the past, being with you was the best thing that ever happened to me…until Aram made me feel like a dirty old man." She jerked at that. He almost kicked himself for bringing it up. He tried to divert her. "Then, from the night we met again—"

She wouldn't be diverted. "How did Aram make you feel like that?" He shrugged. She clung to his arm, ebony eyes entreating, undeniable. "Tell me, please."

How could he resist her when she looked at him that way?

And then, he wanted no secrets between them. Ever again.

He exhaled. "You remember how I used to spend every possible second with you and Aram, either individually or together. Then one day, after a squash match—he'd trounced me, too—I related something clever that you'd said to me the day before, and he tore into me. Called me a cruel, spoiled prince, accused me of ignoring him for years whenever he'd tried to warn me about treating you too indulgently, to stop encouraging your hopeless crush on me. Then he threatened me."

"Wh-what did he threaten you with?"

"Not death or serious injury, don't worry. But that was actually what shook me most—how intense but nonviolent he was. It was as if he hated me, and had for a long time. I would have preferred it if he'd beaten me up, broken a few bones. I would have healed from that. But I never healed from losing his friendship. He told me that if I didn't keep you away from me, he'd make my father order me to never come near you again."

"So that was why you suddenly shunned us!"

He nodded. "I tried to defend myself at first, said you

were the little sister I never had and how dare he say I'd think of you—or encourage you to think of me—*that* way."

"So you never thought of me…that way?"

"No." She seemed dismayed at his emphatic negation. "Come on, Johara, I was a man of twenty-two, you were a kid of fourteen. I would have been a pervert if I had thought of you that way. But you were *my* girl, the only one who 'got' me. I had to explain myself to everyone else, even to Aram and my family, but not to you. I loved you, in every way but *that* way. I love you in every way now."

He poured his emotions into her eyes, then her lips. She surfaced from the mating of their mouths, panting. Then pleasure drained from her face as the pall of what they'd been discussing resurfaced. "What happened after that?"

He sighed again. "Aram said he didn't give a damn what I thought or felt. He only cared that I was emotionally exploiting you. And he couldn't stand by until I damaged you irrevocably. I realized he was doing what he thought best to protect you, which is why I was never really angry at him. Perhaps subconsciously, I *was* waiting for you to grow up so that I could feel that way about you. So in a fit of mortification, I swore I'd never talk to you, *or* him, again, that neither of you would have to put up with the 'cruel, spoiled prince' anymore. That's why I pulled away, in a misguided effort to keep my word to him.

"Then, as I agonized over how much I'd inadvertently hurt my best friends, you left Zohayd, and your father announced that you wouldn't be coming back. My last memory of you was of your forlorn face as you left the palace. I felt I'd betrayed our friendship. I left Zohayd soon afterward, and came back only sporadically through the years, until Aram left Zohayd a few years back. I felt I didn't have the right to try to heal our friendship."

She stared at him, chest heaving, emotions flashing in dizzying succession over her ultra-expressive face.

Then she threw herself at him, crushed him to her. "Ah, *ya habibi,* I'm so sorry. Aram was *so* wrong."

His lips twisted as he looked down at their entwined nakedness. "I think he was *so* right."

"He was wrong *then.* That's what counts. You never led me on, never hurt me. I owe most of what I am today to your friendship. I think I'm not as messed up as he feared I'd be."

"You're perfection itself, inside and out."

"See? He was absolutely wrong. Ooh!" She punched a pillow. "And the rat even told me you said you stopped talking to us because we were 'the help.'"

"What?" he shouted. "All right, *now* I am angry at him."

"Makes two of us. Just wait until I get ahold of him. I'm going to have his overprotective hide!"

"I hope you didn't believe him!"

She slid a leg between his, stroked his face, laying everything inside her wide-open for him to read, to drink deeply of. "Does it look like I did?"

"No, *alhamdulel'lah,* thank God." He stroked her back in wonder. "You're all I want. It's all I want, to be with you."

A grimace wiped away her loving expression. "Wanting it and being able to do it are polar opposites here."

He threaded his fingers through her hair, cupped her head through its thickness, took her lips in a fierce kiss.

"Things might be complicated now, but I will resolve everything—"

"Please, don't. Don't promise me anything. I don't want you burdening yourself with what you can't accomplish, or with the guilt when you fail to. I will take what I can have with you, and I'll always be happy that I did. That I love you. That you love me."

Before he could protest, she dragged him to her, drowned him in delirious passion, taking the reins this time.

In the aftermath of pleasure, she slept in his arms. He remained awake, watching her.

And he knew he couldn't tell her. About the jewels, or about his plan. He couldn't bring the ugliness of the outside world into their happiness now. He wouldn't sully hers if at all possible.

It was up to him to make it so.

For the next two weeks, Johara spent a few hours every morning helping her father pack, resolve any standing issues and train his replacements before she slipped away to Shaheen's villa to throw herself in his arms.

He told her again and again not to worry, that he was working on securing a way for them to be together.

She believed he'd fail. That her time with him was counting down. Again. On a slower scale than that night she'd thought would be all she'd have of him, but counting down still. And when their time ran out, it would break them both.

But she couldn't think of that now. She was bound on filling every second they had left with wonder and happiness and pleasure. Maybe if they charged every cell they could with love and closeness and cherishing, they might be able to endure the desolation of a life without each other.

She opened the front door to his villa, knowing she'd find it empty. He wasn't here. A message ten minutes ago had told her he'd been detained, but would be there soon. And that he adored her.

She sighed in anticipation, soaking up the masculine elegance surrounding her. Acres of polished marble the color of the awe-inspiring beaches just steps from the back porch, whitewashed walls, deep brown furniture the color of the palm trees that seemed to form a natural fortress wall around the villa, and accents in gradations of emerald like the breathtaking sea that greeted her from every window, spreading to the horizon.

"I was told, but I couldn't believe it."

For the moment it took the words to sink into her brain, she had the conviction that Shaheen's voice was the one that caressed her ears and slid down every inch of her skin, his presence that reached out to envelop her.

But even before she spun around, she knew. It was almost Shaheen's voice, almost his presence. But it wasn't him.

This voice had the same beauty and depth and influence, but instead of warmth it held an arctic chill, instead of emotion there was a void. This presence wasn't permeated by humor and gentleness and compassion, but by sarcasm and aggression and cruelty. She knew who it was before she saw him.

Amjad.

Shaheen's oldest brother. The crown prince of Zohayd. One of the most unstoppable forces in the world of finance.

And the most feared man in the region.

Her jaw almost dropped as she watched him approach her with the languid, majestic prowl of a stalking tiger.

This must be what a fallen angel looked like. Impossible beauty, hair-raising aura. His luminescent emerald eyes were said to be the only of their kind in the Aal Shalaan family in five centuries, inherited directly from Ezzat Aal Shalaan, the founder of Zohayd. Many even said Amjad was his replica, with the same imposing physique, frightening intelligence and overwhelming charisma. Some believed he was Ezzat reincarnated.

It was also said their lives followed much the same lines. Ezzat's first wife had also plotted to murder him.

But that was where their destinies diverged. Ezzat had found his true love only a year after aborting the plot against his life, had lived with her in harmony from the time he'd married her at thirty-one till the day he'd died at eighty-five.

Amjad had exposed his treacherous wife eight years ago, and there was no sign that he'd find someone to love. In fact, from what she'd heard, he seemed determined to wrestle destiny into submission, thwarting any of its attempts to bring him any measure of closeness again.

"Now I see that what I thought to be ridiculous hyperbole is actually pathetic understatement. You've become a goddess, Johara."

Johara blinked at Amjad, stunned.

His smile would probably cause a meltdown were any of Zohayd's female population within sight and earshot. But it shocked her to see that predatory sensuality on the face of the man she'd always considered her oldest brother.

Not knowing what to say to that, she said what she did feel. "It's so good to see you, Amjad."

His eyes crinkled, making them even more chilling. "Is it?"

She swallowed, suddenly feeling like a mouse about to be made a bored cat's swatting toy. "Yes, of course. It's been so many years. You're looking well."

"Just well?" Amjad's spectacular lips turned down in a pout. "I usually get a more…enthusiastic response from the ladies."

She cleared her throat. "You know how you look, Amjad. Surely the last thing a man of your caliber needs is an ego stroke."

"Ouch." He winced, looking anything but hurt, the calculation in his eyes growing more cutting. "But then again, an ego stroke from a woman of your caliber is something to be coveted. Any kind of stroke would be… most welcome."

She gaped as he stopped barely a foot away, tried to step back. He stepped forward, maintaining the suffocating nearness.

She, too, had thought the tales she'd heard about him had been exaggerations. They were absolute understatements. This close, she got a good look at what Amjad had become.

It was as if his magnificent body was a shell, housing an entity of overpowering intellect and annihilating disdain. He'd used to be a loving, outgoing, deeply passionate and committed man. The woman who'd tried to poison him might have failed to kill him, but she'd poisoned his soul and killed off everything that had made him the incredible force for good he'd once been.

Regret squeezed her heart.

Suddenly every hair on her body stood on end, in sheer shock.

His hand slid around her waist, tugged her flush against his hardness from breast to knee.

She froze, unable to even breathe.

At last, she choked out, "Amjad, please, don't—"

He pressed her closer. "Don't what, *ya joharti?*"

Hearing Shaheen's endearment for her from anyone else would have startled her. Hearing it from Amjad, spoken with that insolent familiarity, seriously disturbed her.

He didn't disgust her. It was impossible for him to do so; he was Shaheen's flesh and blood. He was like *her* brother, even if he was behaving as anything but. She only felt so sad she wanted to weep. Then she got mad.

She pushed at him with all her strength. "Don't call me that. I'm not your anything."

She could have been fighting a brick wall. His hold didn't even loosen. He even pulled her closer. "Not yet. But I can be. Your everything, if you only say the word. I can give you everything, Johara. Just name it and it's yours."

Mortification washed over her as the full realization of what he was doing here radiated outward, drenching her in a storm of goose bumps. "Please…don't do this."

He caught her hands, dragged her arms around his neck, held them in place with one hand, the other keeping her head prisoner as he swooped down and latched his lips to her exposed neck. She might have cried out, but the next second, thunder drowned out all her efforts.

"*B'haggej'jaheem,* what are you *doing?*"

Eight

Johara's heart stopped the moment Shaheen's enraged voice slammed into her back.

But it wasn't only her heart that plunged into deep freeze. The paralysis was total as Amjad straightened in degrees, not in any hurry to turn to face Shaheen. She could only stare up at him as he raised his head, releasing her neck from the coldness of his lips, which may as well have been draining her life away. Then she met his eyes and the ice encasing her turned to stone as he let her see what he felt toward her for the first time. Sheer abhorrence.

One hand was still locking both of hers around his neck. He brought the other one up and her horror deepened. To any onlooker—to Shaheen—it would seem as if he were unclasping the hands she had clamped there of her own will.

Then Amjad moved aside, affording her a direct look

at Shaheen. He was standing under the arch between the foyer and the expansive sitting area. She would have sobbed if she hadn't been struck mute. She'd never imagined Shaheen looking like that. He looked… frightening.

"Shaheen, you're home early." Amjad turned to his younger brother in a sweep of pure grace and power, unperturbed, imperturbable. "Johara and I were getting…reacquainted."

Inside, she was screaming. *Don't believe him.* Outside, she could only watch his reaction in mounting horror. Then realization descended and she gave up trying to break out of her paralysis.

Maybe this was for the best. Shaheen's best. If he believed Amjad, he'd be hurt, betrayed. But he'd eventually be free of his love for her. Free of her. She wished that for him, the peace and freedom she'd never have.

Shaheen moved then, walked up to them. Even with desperation descending on her, his every step closer thudded in her now stampeding heart like the ticking of a time bomb. And he didn't even meet her eyes. He kept his locked on his older brother's.

Then he stopped, his gaze moving to the arm maintaining a hold on her waist. Without raising his eyes again he said, "Take your hand off Johara, Amjad. Or have every bone in it broken."

She shuddered. His voice was now as pitiless as Amjad's. Worse. Laden with barely contained aggression.

Amjad finally let go of her, raised both hands up in a cross between mock placation and false surrender. "Intense. And here I thought you were gentleman enough not to make this more…awkward than it is. So, little brother, is this your way of laying claim to a woman? Threatening other men off? Afraid if you let her choose which man best fulfills her…needs, she won't choose you? So it is like Johara said. You are leaving her no choice but to succumb to your…attentions."

"One more word and you'll be flat on your back with a broken jaw, spitting out blood and teeth."

"I should have believed you when you told me what a caveman he was being." Amjad's ruthlessly handsome face shifted from chillingly sincere as he addressed her to devilishly goading as he turned to Shaheen. "That was over a dozen words, by the way."

Shaheen pounced, grabbed Amjad by his casual yet superbly cut zippered black sweater. Every nerve in her body slackened as the two majestic forces of nature prepared to collide.

They were equal in every way, so similar, yet seemed like opposites. Even in his fury, Shaheen's spirit shone untarnished, radiating a spectrum of positive vibes and influences, while Amjad's emptiness seemed to suck all light and life from his surroundings, to turn everything dark and hopeless.

After a breathless moment of tension as she trembled with the need to throw herself between them but forced herself to let this unfold without her intervention, with a mutter of disgust, Shaheen pushed Amjad away so hard that his older brother took several steps backward to steady himself.

"You're not worth it," Shaheen hissed.

"Go ahead, make me the villain here. But this was mutual."

Shaheen bared his teeth on a fed-up grimace. "Shut *up*."

"Or what? You've already decided not to sully your

hands with my blood." Amjad straightened his clothes, swept the hair that had rained down his face to frame his slashed cheekbones back in place. "I didn't know you were that involved, but maybe it's for the best. You really have to be objective, Shaheen. A woman has a right to look out for her best interests. Johara is justified in looking out for number one and going out *for* number one. And let's face it. With your problems, you don't make the grade."

Shaheen gave a vicious snort. "Save your venom, Amjad, even if you have an unlimited supply of it. You must be far less shrewd and insightful than I gave you credit for if you believe for a second I'm buying this farce you staged."

Amjad gave him a pitying glance. "Is that what you're hoping this is? Something I staged? How would I have staged her arms around me when you walked in?"

"Knowing you, you bulldozed her into it. Knowing her, she was too considerate of who you are—to me, and to her in the past—to blast you off the face of the earth as you deserve." Shaheen suddenly seemed to think Amjad deserved no more attention, swung to her, his face transforming in a heartbeat from intolerant and unforgiving to the very sight of tenderness and concern. "I'm so sorry, *ya joharet galbi,* that I exposed you to this indignity."

Overwhelmed, she whispered, "You didn't do anything…"

"It is on my account that Amjad has insulted you, in an effort to plant doubt in my mind about your feelings and intentions toward me."

"You realized what he… You know that I…" She choked, unable to go on. That he trusted her, didn't even pause to question…

All thought of giving him up for his own good forgotten, she threw herself into his arms, breath gone, her heart fracturing at his feet from too much love. He soothed her with gentle caresses, his words of love and apology unceasing. "I'll always know what's in your heart. You *are* my heart."

"My, Shaheen…" Amjad's sarcasm fractured their moment of communion. "This has to set a new world record for patheticness. Think, little brother. Why is she back now of all times? Contrary to you, she knows you're not as clever as you think you are, that we were bound to find out about your 'secret' arrangement."

Shaheen turned to Amjad, never loosening his hold on her. "We? You mean Father knows, too?"

Amjad gave a denigrating huff. "With the hoops you're making him hop through and the condition he's been in since Aliyah and Anna returned? Nah. But if *I* put his and hers together when I saw her coming back to the palace all flushed and flustered yesterday while you were pointedly away, I'm sure others of lesser insight will catch on and connect the dots."

Shaheen shook his head in amazement. "So enlighten me, Amjad. What is Johara's plan, in your opinion?"

Amjad sighed as if he had to explain that things fell down or water was wet to a moron. "She's after a ransom. Yours. I was pretending to offer her myself in return for unhooking you from her claws when you interrupted."

Shaheen massaged her waist, as if to erase Amjad's accusations and disdain. "But I didn't interrupt. You dragged me away on a wild-goose chase, waited for Johara, timed your performance so I'd walk in to see her presumably in your arms. And you thought I'd charge in and accuse her of betraying me."

Amjad looked the image of uncaring boredom. "Would have been less…traumatic for you lovebirds if you had. Pity. I gave 'nice' a shot. I should have stuck with my forte—nasty. Now I will."

"First, you'll do nothing, Amjad. Second, if Johara wanted to be bribed to leave gullible me alone, why do you think she insisted on all this secrecy?"

Amjad gave him a ridiculing look. "Because letting you loose when you believe she walks on water will fetch a far higher price. And it worked. I was willing to pay top dollar."

Shaheen only laughed at that, looked down at her, no longer seething with affront, but highly entertained. "What would it cost for you to let go of me, *ya joharti?"*

A smile twisted with a wince on her lips. "You know."

Shaheen stilled them in a fierce kiss before he looked back at Amjad. "Only I can make her let go of me, Amjad. And I'm never letting her go. So why don't you get down on your knees and beg Johara's forgiveness, then get out of here?"

Amjad huffed in disgust. "She really has you clinging around her pinky with your face smashed against it, doesn't she? Fine. Every man has a right to choose his poison. But risking war for her? Tsk."

"If you're so concerned about war, why don't you do something about it? Break your pathetic vow never to marry again and take one of those brides they want to shove down my throat."

"Oh, I did break it, when I saw you kicking and screaming. I thought as crown prince they'd jump at my offer. But father came back to me with the consensus within an hour. No bride will have me. They believe

I'll go all Shahrayar or Othello on them. Even if their families are willing to sacrifice their daughters at the altar of my madness, the families think I'll turn on the next of kin. Comes from being viewed as a force that can't be approached let alone harnessed and profited from, I guess."

Shaheen guffawed. "Aw, thanks for trying to spare me *that* at least. But I'm so glad you're not shocked that you were turned down. You *have* been tearing through the kingdom—and the world—with borderline sane actions and insane gambles."

Amjad's gaze grew more ridiculing. "Really? Then how has each one paid off big-time? Maybe I'm not as irrational as you all like to think I am. Digest this and gain new insight into your mad brother's actions and convictions. You'll find I'm right about other things, too." He flicked Johara a just-wait-until-I'm-through-with-you look. "Her, for instance. Even if you can't think so now, being caught in her love spell."

Johara saw Shaheen's eyes soften. "It's you who are under a spell—of hatred. You knew and loved Johara once, too. Yet you can't access that knowledge or that love because of the paranoia you've been trapped in since Salmah. You will never understand that I'd mistrust myself before I would Johara. I trust her with my life, and far more."

Amjad pretended to dust himself off. "Yuck. All that sticky nonsense will take some heavy-duty sense to wash off. Well, you go ahead and smother yourself in her honey trap for now, while I—"

He stopped, turned his head. Then she, too, heard what had caught his attention. A faraway drone. It was getting louder, nearer by the second. In moments, it was unmistakable.

A helicopter.

Amjad turned back, derision turning his beauty into that of an unrepentant devil. "Uh-oh. Sounds like the cavalry have realized what you're up to and are charging here to save you from your mushy heart and malfunctioning mind."

Giving him one last impatient look, Shaheen clasped her hand and led her to the western veranda, where she noticed for the first time a clearance that must be a launching/landing pad.

It was. In seconds, the helicopter landed there. As the rotors winded down, a very tall, broad man jumped down from the pilot's side. He rushed to the passenger's side to help a woman down, his movements as tender as Shaheen's were with her. She worked out the woman's identity when she recognized the man. Kamal Aal Masood, the king of Judar.

Sure enough, Aliyah came into view, proving Johara's deduction. And deepening her agitation.

From the grim expression on Aliyah's face as she approached the villa with her juggernaut of a husband, Johara knew that her reason for interrupting them the other night hadn't been resolved. And Johara was certain that it concerned her. Probably Amjad's same concern. And Aliyah was back to broach the subject with Shaheen, with a one-man army as reinforcement.

The regal couple walked into the villa. Shaheen received them with her at his side, hugging them both and introducing her to Kamal. Kamal gallantly kissed her hand. Aliyah gave her the accustomed three kisses, one on one cheek, two on the other. It all seemed genial enough, but Johara vibrated with the tension radiating from the couple, from the whole scene.

Amjad advanced on them, pulled Aliyah in for a

quick kiss, thumped Kamal on the back, then got to the point without preamble, breaking the stilted cordiality. "So, Kamal, what warrants the presence of the king of Judar on our soil and on such a clandestine visit, too?"

Kamal gave Amjad a smile that echoed his own, that of a man who knew his own power to its last iota, was versed in wielding it to its most destructive limits, who tolerated nothing but his own way, always. "So which part of 'clandestine' don't you get, Amjad?"

Aliyah arched an exquisite eyebrow at him. "Yes, Amjad, if we wanted you to be involved, we wouldn't have come here."

Amjad held a hand to his heart as if Aliyah had shot him there with a barb. "Whoa. My little cousin-turned-sister has grown some sharp fangs. Especially with your weapon-of-mass-destruction husband at hand."

Kamal coughed a laugh. "If you think she's baring her fangs because I'm here, then you should be reintroduced to your little cousin-turned-sister. I'm the one who holds her back when she wants to rip you to shreds. You remind her too much of me before she…unscrambled me."

Amjad gave him a look of mock sweetness, belittlment blaring in it. "Yes, I can see you're all 'fixed.'"

Aliyah harrumphed. "You should be so lucky to find someone who'd 'fix' you, too, Amjad."

"How about I pass, sis? For the next few reincarnations."

Kamal stepped nearer, his smile becoming as confrontational as Amjad's was disparaging. "How about I 'fix' you myself?"

Amjad's smile grew more provoking. He was clearly spoiling for the fight Shaheen had denied him. "That's how you get your kicks nowadays, Kamal? You can't win against the lady who has you whipped, so you pick fights to win her lenience? Shaheen just finished attempting the same thing, by the way."

"You know, Amjad, I've been wanting to deck you for a long time. Now is as good a time as any to finally act on the impulse."

As the two men squared off, Johara found herself absently thinking they could have been brothers, too. And it wasn't just their height and looks. Kamal had more in common with Amjad than Shaheen did. There was the same harshness about him, chiseled into his face and carved into his being. This man could be ruthless. Must regularly be so, to be able to govern Zohayd's big sister kingdom so well, to be obeyed so completely in this volatile region.

Aliyah pushed the two men apart, one hand perpendicular to the other. "Okay, testosterone timeout. In your corners, boys."

Johara blinked at the transformation that came over Kamal as he looked at Aliyah. It was a shock to see softness melting him, love and devotion possessing his every feature and move. Johara recognized the emotions that she and Shaheen shared. She had no doubt Aliyah was everything to Kamal, that he'd die for her. And vice versa.

Kamal gave Aliyah a loving squeeze. "Just because you wish it, *ya rohi.* But next time you want to shred him, let me know."

Amjad snorted. "So apart from airing the fond fantasies you all have of beating me up, can I hope you're here on an undercover mission to save Shaheen from his stupidity, too?"

Kamal's lips twisted. "Maybe I'm here to show him

some youngest-brother solidarity, sharing my expertise in swatting off nuisance older brothers."

"You mean Farooq and Shehab?" Amjad huffed. "Those softies who left you the throne to be with their sweethearts? I almost feel it's my duty to coach them in how to make your life harder. You have it way too easy." At Aliyah's jab in his gut, Amjad rolled his eyes, exhaled. "Fine. Keep your regal secrets. For now. I'll leave you foursome to your sickeningly sweet double date." He nodded at Johara as a parting shot. "I'll be watching you."

The other three bristled. Johara almost blurted out that he wouldn't have to, not for long. But Shaheen hugged her closer to him, his protective gesture deepening her muteness.

As soon as Amjad was out of earshot, strolling nonchalantly to the door, Kamal gave a heavy exhalation. "We came here for an update on the progress of your plan and to give you our input, but…" He paused, looked apologetically at Aliyah then Shaheen. "I know I promised, and Amjad is a world-class and probably one-of-a-kind pain, but he's an extensively powerful one, not to mention he's got a major stake in this. Though I agree secrecy is paramount, I do believe he and Harres should be brought in now, not later. We need them."

Shaheen's eyes flared with alarm. "I need more time. My plan is working. I'm gathering more information every day."

Kamal shook his head, emphatic, final. "It's not working well enough or fast enough, Shaheen, and you know it."

"What plan?" Johara clutched Shaheen's arm, her heart thudding with dread. "What's going on, Shaheen?"

Shaheen looked down at her, entreaty setting his eyes ablaze. "It's nothing to concern yourself with, *ya habibati."*

Aliyah placed her hand on his other arm. "No, Shaheen. I now believe Johara has nothing to do with this. And since she doesn't, she needs to know. This involves her, too, as much as or even more than it does any of us."

Johara's heart almost uprooted itself as she watched Shaheen close his eyes for a long moment, confusion and worst-case scenarios crashing through her mind.

Then he let out a ragged exhalation. "Fine. Call Amjad back."

In moments, Kamal walked back with Amjad. Before Amjad could voice the speculation evident on his face, Shaheen began to talk.

Johara could only stare at him as he revealed shock after shock. The jewels. The Pride of Zohayd. Stolen. Replaced by fakes. She filled in the blanks he left out with all present intimately aware of them. The projected consequences.

After he finished talking, the only thing that could do the ominous revelations justice descended on their quintet. Decimating silence. Even Amjad was lost for words.

It was she, who'd been practically mute since Shaheen had walked in, who finally found her voice, a chafing whisper. "Why didn't you tell me?"

Shaheen cupped her cheek, concern seizing his face. "I didn't want to burden you with this before I discovered the culprits."

"Give me a break!" Amjad erupted. "I can forgive you being blind when it's your own life at stake, even if your actions could cause an internal crisis. But civil war pales in comparison to what this could mean to the whole region. Can you even imagine the instability a coup and a new ruling house in Zohayd would cause? Can you even project what could be far worse, a new 'democratic' dictatorship sprouting in the middle of the kingdoms? Are you totally out of your mind? What culprits are you trying to discover? One is standing right before you, the only one who had the opportunity and the means to carry this out. What more do you need? A Dear John videotaped gloating confession from her after she's destroyed us all?"

"I swear I *will* knock you down, Amjad," Shaheen growled.

"Have at it, Shaheen." Amjad threw his hands in the air, calculation gone, agitation taking hold. "I thought Johara's return was the plot of a woman out to get all she can out of the royal family she grew up among. But this is far worse. It's clear how it all happened. Berj summoned her to help him stage his plan and faked his heart attack as motive to call her back. He must have sent her after you to guarantee that no one would think to question her return, not with her double-pronged alibi of being the distraught daughter and hopeless lover. It would have worked spectacularly if Aliyah hadn't discovered the theft."

Shaheen slammed both palms flat into Amjad's shoulders, shouted at him, "You see betrayal everywhere, Amjad. You're so poisoned by it you can't hear how your suspicions cancel each other out. One moment you think Berj and Johara are so stupid they'd do something like this when they'd be the first the fingers point to, the next you accuse them of being consummate manipulators. *You're* the one who's so blind you don't see how flimsy the circumstantial evidence against them is, and the frame up it all reeks of."

"That makes the most sense," Aliyah agreed. "Someone thought Berj and Johara would be the perfect fall guys if the plot was discovered."

"If Aliyah's—and Shaheen's—instincts say you and your father are innocent—" Kamal looked at Johara, a pledge glittering in his golden eyes "—then that's my proof that you are. You have my word I'll do everything in my power to defend you, to discover those who sought to frame you, and to punish them for it."

Amjad put both hands up. "Since the voice of sanity is having no effect in breaking up this mutual admiration society, I'll do more than any of you is willing to even consider. I'll concede that I may have gotten it wrong. But in case I didn't, consider the consequences you might be inviting, chasing fictional culprits while letting the real ones get away. With the jewels, the throne and the region's stability."

"Your concern is noted, Amjad," Shaheen muttered. "And dismissed. Now give me your word you will not go after either Johara or Berj in any way."

Amjad held his brother's eyes for one last moment, before he shrugged. "I can only promise you this—once Harres is brought up to speed, if he believes the same as you, since you're the one who has more to lose than any of us, I'll let you steer this."

Shaheen gave him a curt nod. "Good enough for me."

Aliyah spoke then, in what felt like a summation. "Now that we're not fighting amongst ourselves, I don't think we can be careful enough handling this. Even though the thieves know we wouldn't be able to conduct an open investigation if we did discover the fakes, giving them the false security of believing we haven't will help us uncover them and retrieve the jewels before the Exhibition Ceremony."

After that, the men and Aliyah determined the measures each of them would undertake in the investigation, with Kamal, as the most neutral party, chosen to be the one to inform Harres.

Johara stood by Shaheen, numb, as they departed.

After the last echo of Aliyah's and Kamal's helicopter and Amjad's roaring sports car faded in the distance, Johara remained staring blindly into nothingness.

She'd thought she'd already imagined the worst that could happen, thought she'd done everything she could to protect Shaheen from any consequences. She knew nothing…

She jumped as Shaheen's hands came down on her shoulders. "Come inside from the chill, *ya galbi.* You need to sit down and I need to help you digest it all."

As she nodded, she heard another rumble in the distance. In seconds, she saw what it was. A procession of imposing stretch limos gleaming black in the declining sun, each flaunting Zohayd's gold and emerald flag on its hood.

Shaheen stiffened. "This is all I need to top off this day. Father." He turned to her. "Please, wait in our room. I'll sort this out, whatever it is, as soon as I can."

She could only nod and turn like an automaton to do his bidding.

In minutes, she was sitting on the edge of his bed—theirs for now—every nerve in her body jerking at each sound as she documented the cavalcade's movements, the voices she distinguished to be Shaheen's and his father's rising, then the sound of urgent footsteps up the stairs, coming nearer and nearer.

The door to Shaheen's bedroom burst open.

Shaheen stood behind his father looking like he might shove the king out of the way. Then King Atef, in full royal garb, advanced into the expansive room, dismissing his son's protests.

She rose from the bed, feeling she was about to receive the ultimate blow. Then the king delivered it.

"Is it true, Johara? Are you pregnant with Shaheen's child?"

Nine

Shaheen stared at the back of his father's head, the question reverberating in his mind. His gaze moved to settle on Johara's frozen face. Her eyes were holding his father's, shocked denial filling them.

Then she quavered, "No, I'm not."

And he got his confirmation.

Johara *was* pregnant.

He felt his heart spiral inside him, as if he were plummeting down a never-ending roller coaster.

From the moment he'd found her gone, he'd wondered if there'd been consequences to their surrender to passion without a thought for precautions. Thinking she could discover her pregnancy while she was alone had exacerbated his misery at her disappearance. But she'd said nothing since they'd been together again, making him certain she wasn't pregnant. Then after that first time when she'd stopped him from using precautions, making him believe she'd taken her own, they'd made love again and again through the past two weeks, and he'd believed there was no chance of their passion bearing fruit.

But she hadn't taken precautions because she was already pregnant. And she hadn't told him due to her seemingly unwavering decision to never compromise him or impose on him with demands she believed she had no right to make, and that he'd be incapable of meeting.

From what felt like the bottom of an abyss he heard his father's voice, thickened with regret and apology.

"I'm sorry, *ya b'nayti,* if I'm relieved to hear that. I couldn't wish for a better woman for Shaheen, but as king, the last thing I can consider are my wishes. With the current situation and Shaheen's commitment to defusing the brewing unrest, I am forced to consider only that, at whatever cost to myself and my family."

Shaheen saw Johara nod, her golden hair a gentle wave of resignation around her face. And he moved, pushed past his father.

He stopped before her. Unable to touch her as his emotions mushroomed, he heard a bass rumble bleed out of him. "You didn't believe me. When I pledged that we would be together, that I am yours and will never be anyone else's. And this is why you never told me. You were planning on leaving me 'to my destiny' without telling me. You planned to have our baby on your own."

She cast her eyes down, as if to misdirect him from the knowledge now coursing through his blood, as if he needed to look into her eyes to see through to her soul. "I s-said I'm not pregnant."

He touched her then, just a finger below her chin,

bringing up those eyes that he needed to look into to feel alive now. "Yes, because you're terminally heroic and misguided and want to sacrifice yourself for my so-called best interests and those of Zohayd. Your eyes are still promising me freedom, when my only freedom is to be yours."

His father advanced, confusion and foreboding warring over his weathered, noble face. "So, is it true?"

Johara held Shaheen's eyes, the attempt to hide the truth trembling for one last moment before it fractured. And it came flooding out with a cascade of beseeching tears. "I'm sorry…"

He snatched her into his arms, crushed her to him. "Be sorry only for hiding this from me, for thinking of denying me not only you, but our child, too. Don't you understand I'd rather die than be without you?"

"I would, too." She sobbed in his chest. "But I never wanted to cause you trouble. Now I've caused you nothing but. Oh, Shaheen, I shouldn't have come to that party…"

He held her away to scowl his exasperation down on her. "And what am I? A boy with no will of my own, who didn't realize the consequences of my actions? Everything I did, I'd do again in the exact same way. The only thing I'd change would be to tie you to my wrist so you wouldn't leave me for my 'own good,' so I'd be there to celebrate the discovery of your pregnancy with you." Anger at her efforts to protect him frothed on a new surge. "You slept in my arms every day, told me everything…but *that.* Would you have ever told me?"

"No." Her eyes melted with entreaty. "I never wanted to keep this from you, but I can't think beyond the moment with you, can't imagine a time when you'll no

longer be part of my life or that you won't be part of our baby's. All I know is that my pregnancy will do what the king is saying it will. I can't even imagine the damages if people know you have an heir on the way."

"And the damages to us, to our baby? You didn't imagine those?"

A rumble penetrated their cocoon of agitation. Shaheen turned to look at his father, winced at the mess of love and regret and finality that congealed on his face.

Then in a voice heavy with them all, the king said, "I am beyond happy that you have a woman you want—"

Shaheen interrupted him. "I *love* Johara. Always have, always will. There will be no negotiations about that."

His father continued, a king who wouldn't let even his son, or his pain on his behalf, stop him from seeing his duty through. "That this woman is Johara makes it infinitely better. But there is no stopping the chain reaction this will set off." He turned to Johara, gaze heavy with the remorse of being unable to put her before everything. "News of your pregnancy came to me through servants, so it must be all over the region by now. All we can do is rewrite history and hope for the least possible consequences."

Johara darted a look into Shaheen's eyes before her gaze went back to his father. "What do you mean?"

His father exhaled raggedly. "I will announce that you're already married in a *zawaj orfi*. Even if it is a secret marriage and frowned upon—and in royal circles in Zohayd, unprecedented—it remains binding. We'll say this is why you followed Shaheen to Zohayd after such a long absence. It will legitimize your baby, and we'll have a marriage ritual to make the marriage public and fully legal."

Shaheen felt Johara tremble in his arms, saw hope quiver on her face before doubt snuffed it out again. "What about the marriage of state Shaheen is required to enter? How will this affect your negotiations and peace in Zohayd?"

His father's shoulder slumped lower. "I'll try to convince any tribe to consent to giving their daughter as a second wife."

Shaheen had known what the condition to his father's damage control solution could be. It still outraged him to hear it. "They can consent all they like. *I'm* not taking a second wife."

"Don't be so quick to dismiss this option, Shaheen."

"I never intended to marry anyone but Johara. I was only biding my time until—" Shaheen stopped. He'd almost blurted out the reason he'd appeared to be going along with the negotiations "—until I found a way out with the least repercussions. But now that I've seen the price I could have paid for not confronting this, I'm no longer pretending."

"What choice do we have, Shaheen? If you don't meet them halfway at least, there will be fallout into the next century. I would have given anything apart from the kingdom's peace for you to have Johara. But no matter what happens now, you'll at least have your child, raise it as your own, and not be deprived of it as I was deprived of Aliyah until lately."

"Are you even listening to yourself, Father? You sacrificed your one true love and ended up thinking your daughter was your niece, and only because *Ammeti* Bahiyah rescued her from a life of anonymity. But what did your sacrifices ever gain you, or the kingdom? You've been battling one potential uprising after another ever since, the last one two years ago when only Aliyah's and Kamal's marriage defused it at the last moment. And here they are, threatening another, and you think sacrificing me will appease them? For how long? They're like tantrum-throwing brats and the more you give them the more they'll demand and the louder they'll scream for it. You can never placate them. So I'm marrying Johara now, not later as I was determined to. And not as a damage-control measure, but because being with her is the one thing I've ever wanted for myself. And I will be with her for the rest of my life. You and the rest of the tribes must deal with it."

Johara clung to him. "I can't let you do that to yourself and your father and kingdom, Shaheen. Not on my account—"

"It's on all our accounts—yours, mine and our baby's. Trust me, *ya joharet galbi.* I will resolve this."

Her fingers dug into his arms, her eyes unwavering with determination. "Then promise me…if you can't, you'll let me go."

"I promise I never will."

Before she could protest more, his father spoke, his voice like a knell of doom. "Don't make promises you can't afford to keep, Shaheen." Before Shaheen could interrupt, his father forged on. "Now you will come back to the palace with me. Your marriage ceremony must be arranged at once."

"My deepest admiration, Johara, from one master manipulator to another. You're the very best I've seen."

Johara stiffened at Amjad's drawling sneer. Shaheen

gave her a bolstering squeeze before he turned to his brother.

It was Harres, who'd met them at the palace's main entrance, who answered him. "It was I who recommended you be one of the two witnesses to the marriage, Amjad. I can easily replace you with Father. Or anyone off the street."

"And deprive me of the pleasure of handing Shaheen over to the lioness he's so eager to be devoured by? Can you be so cruel?" Amjad put his arm around Shaheen's shoulder, looked Johara in the eyes. "So how do you think Johara leaked the info about her pregnancy? She must be rubbing her hands in glee that it created the desired scandal and results. You aren't the only one who can't wait for you to marry her now. Everyone—including me—is shoving you at her."

Shaheen looked heavenward before leveling pitying eyes on him. "Do you drink two cups of hot paranoia first thing each morning?"

Amjad cracked a laugh, gave him a hard tug before letting him go. "I bet they have better taste and effect than the cups of insipid sentimentality you're guzzling down nonstop."

"Then how about you try a sip of common, if rare to you, sense?" Shaheen said. "The palace is crawling with aides whose favorite pastime is to monitor the palace's inmates, and who have nothing but sex scandals on the brain. A female versed in signs of early pregnancy must have guessed Johara's condition and put the same 'his and hers' together that you did and spread the word. Father's *kabeer el yaweran* thought the rumor too dangerous to ignore and relayed it. Happy now?"

"Ecstatic." Amjad folded one hand on top of the

other over his heart in mock delight. "I'm going to be an uncle!"

Shaheen grimaced. "In theory. In practice, I'm not letting you near your niece or nephew if you don't revert to being human."

"You mean I ever was one? Flatterer. But I'll leave humanity to you. With all the associated stupidities of the condition. Which, I admit, have most entertaining facets. It was very enlightening to learn that you don't care about sending the region to hell in a handcart as long as you have Johara and your impending offspring. Such a relief to know you're not perfect after all, Shaheen. I was beginning to really worry about you."

Shaheen only gave him a serene look. "So, any new accusations for Johara and her father, Amjad? Get them all off your chest."

Amjad shrugged his shoulders, which were immaculately draped in a navy silk shirt. "Oh, just variations on the old themes according to the developments." He turned his gaze to Johara. "She's full of surprises, isn't she, our Johara?"

Harres punched him in the arm, pointed two fingers to his own eyes. "You keep your eyes here, *faahem?*"

Amjad massaged away his brother's punch, his grin goading. "I understand. You're now one of Johara's lackeys."

Harres narrowed his eyes. "I *can* order my special forces to take you someplace where you can stew in your poisonous brew until the ceremony is over."

"You think they'd obey you and not their crown prince? I'm almost tempted to let you see where their loyalties lie."

"I'll say it's on grounds of insanity. You've paved

those, so it won't be hard to convince them to cart you away."

"But-but…mo-*om!*" Amjad did a spectacular impression of a sullen boy and it only made Johara think she'd never been in the presence of someone more dangerous. Or more…lonely. "I'm the only fun one around. What would this party be without me?"

Harres shook his head, intense fondness mixing with exasperation and even regret. "I swear, sometimes I feel you're the youngest, not the oldest."

Amjad's provocation rose another notch. "But you remain stuck in the middle either way, bro."

"You *said* you'd defer to my opinion. I should have known you would only if it coincided with yours." Harres turned to Johara with long-suffering apology in his eyes. "I told Amjad that his theories of you being behind the jewel conspiracy and creating a scandal to force Shaheen to marry you cancel each other out. If the conspiracy bore fruit, Shaheen wouldn't be prince. Why sabotage the status Amjad thinks you're marrying him for?"

Amjad raised his hand in another impression of an overeager student in class. "I know that one!" Johara turned reluctant eyes to him. The man was electrically charismatic even when he insulted her with every breath. He met her eyes, and still talked about her as if she wasn't there. "It's a win-win situation for her. If the conspiracy works, she gets paid off big-time, Shaheen loses the title but retains his wealth and power as a businessman and sheikh, and she retains her chokehold on him in every way. Then, once she has all power in her hands, she negotiates the return of the jewels, at whatever price, through a third party, and has it all."

Harres gave a hearty snort. "Sheesh, Amjad. You

actually live with that thing you call a brain inside your head?"

"You envy me because you live with nothing inside yours? That must be how our head of homeland security and secret service got to be so trusting. I almost feel compelled to report this to the council. I bet they'd expel you from your post and toss you out on your ear if they got a whiff of you being such an oblivious romantic."

Shaheen grinned at him. "Crown prince or not, Amjad, we outnumber you. How about we throw you out on *your* ear?"

Amjad swept his brothers a bedeviling smile, so secure in his power that he couldn't be goaded into posturing. "Chill, boys. Haven't you ever heard of the esteemed position of devil's advocate?"

"You mean devil's assistant." Harres tsked. "Now of all times. You're sick, Amjad."

"I'll live. But really, when better? Afterward, I'll have to forever hold my aggression. And with Shaheen thinking with body parts that don't include his brain, you were my last hope of someone seeing beyond the star-crossed drama unfolding here."

At that moment the king called Shaheen and Harres away, leaving Amjad alone with Johara.

She waited until they were out of earshot. Then she pounced.

She grabbed Amjad's forearm, dug her fingers into it with all her strength. She heard his surprise in the sharpness of his indrawn breath, saw it in the pupils that jerked to full expansion, engulfing the uncanny emerald of his eyes.

"Listen, Amjad," she hissed. "I'm not in any condition to listen to more of your delightful theories about my cunning and long-term treachery. I've loved Shaheen since the moment I laid eyes on him, even before he saved my life. I thought living with my hopeless love was the worst thing that I'd ever feel. Then I came back into his life and realized he's loved me as long and as fiercely, and my pain became agony. I feel like I've fallen into a nightmare, getting my impossible dream of having Shaheen, but in this terrible way. All I have to look forward to is a few months with him, if that, then a life without him, when he'll love and need me and our baby as much as we do him, but be forced to live without us.

"So thank your demons that *you've* never loved like this and evidently *can't* love anyone. You'll never suffer the agonies and ecstasies of our soul-deep connection, or the despair I'm anticipating when I have to leave him. And I'm *not* letting you add to his troubles. So, to quote Shaheen, from now on, Amjad, shut *up!*"

She fell silent, glaring up at him, trembling with the emotions tearing through her, and thought if stupefaction took human form, it would be Amjad now.

When he remained silent, she let out the air in her lungs on a choppy exhalation. "Now take your mind off of me and concentrate those formidable powers of yours on the most important thing. The jewels."

He shook his head, as if to wake up from a trance. Then he finally drawled, "It has always paid for me to think the worst and make amends later if need be. So I will do anything I can to atone for my attitude when—*and if*—I become convinced you are innocent." He bent closer, as if to give her a mind and psyche scan. "So just answer me this, Johara—if you and your father *are* innocent, why didn't you recognize the fakes?"

"I know why." Johara jerked around at Shaheen's declaration. He and Harres reached her and Amjad's side again. "Berj has been sliding into depression, and his inability to focus on his job—and therefore his failure to notice the fakes—is the reason he's retiring. Johara hasn't been near the jewels since she left Zohayd twelve years ago."

Amjad pursed his lips as he considered those rationalizations. "I still need to interrogate Berj."

Shaheen exhaled. "The one thing saving you from a right hook to that implacable jaw of yours is that I don't want to put a swollen hand in Johara's during the marriage ceremony."

"I can be your witness with swollen knuckles." Harres's feral eyes flashed on a mixture of sheer deviltry and pure danger.

Amjad whistled in mock admiration. "My, aren't you two full of fine male aggression. Down boys. I'm going to question him as a legitimate party in the investigation, not as a suspect."

Johara intercepted any reaction from Shaheen or Harres, stuck her face in Amjad's. "You can interrogate *me* all you like, but don't you dare go near my father."

"We need him to examine the fakes," Amjad persisted.

Johara shook her head emphatically. "*I'll* do that."

"Are you qualified?" She glared at him. He raised his hands in concession. "So you are. Fine. What's your plan?"

"I'll analyze the craftsmanship and come up with a list of possible forgers. There is a limited number of artists in the world capable of producing such almost undetectable duplicates. I've studied each extensively and can distinguish their signature styles."

After Shaheen and Harres agreed that this was the best plan, Amjad stepped closer, curved his arm at her.

She blinked up at him. What was this confounding man up to now?

"What are you up to now?" Shaheen echoed her suspicion.

Amjad eyes crinkled at him on what seemed to be an actual smile. "Johara needs to choose the jewels she'll wear for your wedding. And since you, as her groom, are forbidden to see her from now till then—" Amjad looked at her "—I'm petitioning that she bestow the honor of escorting her to the vaults on me."

After a long moment of stunned silence, Harres guffawed. "Wonders will never cease."

Shaheen seemed to wrestle with indecision before he nodded to her to accept Amjad's offer. He still put a protective hand on top of the one she hooked in Amjad's arm, giving his brother a hard glare. "If you say one more word to upset her..."

"Don't worry, Shaheen." Amjad winked at her. "When I called Johara a lioness, I didn't know the half of it. She can evidently defend herself, and you, against a whole army."

"I heard you wore black for your wedding."

Aliyah laughed at Johara's comment, turned from sorting through the outfits that had been brought in for Johara to pick from. "My choice of the color of mourning and power in Judar was my way of showing Kamal what I thought of being forced into marriage. His, uh, *very* favorable reaction was an early sign that we *are* made for each other." Aliyah stopped, alarmed. "Don't tell me you're thinking of copying me!"

"Oh, no. I just hope you don't expect me to wear white." Johara ran palms down her still flat belly. "It would feel funny when everyone knows we're getting married because I'm pregnant."

"You're getting married because you're in love." That was Laylah, already dressed in the outfit she'd attend the ceremony in, a two-piece dream of gleaming satin and ethereal chiffon in gradations of emerald and turquoise, heavily worked in sequins, beads and pearls. "Don't let the circumstances fool you."

Johara conveyed her gratitude with a look. Laylah and Aliyah had been with her all morning, defusing her agitation at the upcoming events. Not that she'd ever visualized her and Shaheen's wedding, since she'd never thought there would be one, but she'd barely slept all night, dreading the stilted, subdued ceremony that *would* see them married.

Now it was only two hours away. And she still couldn't bring herself to pick a dress. She shook her head at yet another suggestion of Aliyah's.

Aliyah sighed as she put the outfit back on the packed rack. "You're right. None of these are...*you*."

"Maybe you should attend the ceremony wearing only your jewels." Laylah winked at her. "Who needs clothes when she's adorned in the priceless pieces of the Pride of Zohayd?"

Aliyah exchanged a glance with Johara. Laylah hadn't been told.

Before more could be said, a knock rapped on the door of Johara's suite, where she'd insisted on remaining until after the ceremony.

Aliyah rushed to answer the door.

After a moment, she swung around with eyes and smile practically tap-dancing in excitement. "Close your eyes, Johara!"

"What…?" Johara said dazedly, eyes widening instead.

Laylah rushed behind the couch Johara was sitting on and placed her hands over her eyes.

"They're closed," she called out to Aliyah.

After moments of hearing the giggles of the two women, Aliyah chirped "Ta-da!" and Laylah removed her hands.

Johara blinked. Then she gaped. And gaped.

Held high in Aliyah's hand was the most incredible outfit she'd ever seen in her life. And in her line of work, she'd seen the best that human creativity and craftsmanship could offer.

"Now *that's* you," Aliyah announced proudly. "Courtesy of the man who knows you best and values you most, your smitten groom. It has a note attached, too."

That ended Johara's paralysis. She zoomed up and pounced on the truly invaluable part of this gift, the thoughtfulness behind it. Her hands trembled and her eyes surged with tears as she saw Shaheen's elegant, powerful print, almost heard him whisper the words into her ear, against her cheek, her lips, each inch of her.

Lan ustatee abaddan ann oteeki ma yoofi jamalek huqqun, fahal turdeen an ta'khothi nafsi kollaha awadan, ya joharet hayati?

I can never give you what will do your beauty justice, so will you accept taking all of me instead, jewel of my life?

She was useless for an indeterminate time afterward as Aliyah and Laylah surrounded her, sharing her agitated delight.

Then Laylah finally pulled back. "If you *don't* want

to attend your wedding in only jewels, you better hop into that miracle."

And miracle was right. One of every gradation of gold and brown that reflected her coloring down to the last hair, amalgamated from finest silk, georgette, chiffon, lace and tulle, flowing into a three-piece outfit that she molded into as if it had been sculpted for her, on her.

Aliyah and Laylah commented that that was the doing of another miracle. A man who knew every inch of his woman, and who could translate that intimate knowledge into such a precise fit.

Burning with embarrassment and joy, Johara rushed to the full-length mirror to inspect herself, unable to even guess how Shaheen had managed to get this outfit, and on such short notice, too.

She'd worn incredible dresses since she'd turned sixteen, but this one wasn't only her, this was the best her she could be.

The top was corsetlike, accentuating the nip of her waist and the lushness of her breasts, with tiny sleeves and a deep décolleté that showcased the clarity of her complexion and the wonder of each piece of jewelry she wore on her neck and arms.

The jacquard *lehenga* skirt was gathered to one side, hugging her hips in upward sweeps before falling in tight pleats to the floor. The embroidery and cutwork was on a level she'd never seen before, in sequins, silk thread, pearls and gemstones, all Zohaydan traditional motifs built around the first letter of both her name and Shaheen's in Arabic, boggling her mind more, since it proved this had been made in the past twenty-four hours specifically for her. The finishing touch was a flowing silk and chiffon *dupatta* with the same motifs scalloping its edge and that hung from the middle of her head, secured there with a tiara that would have been worth a queen's ransom had it been authentic.

She stood there as the picture was completed, her pleasure at the beauty of it all dipping then dissipating.

All this for such a sterile ceremony.

"It's time, Johara."

She shook off her dejection, rushed to precede Laylah and Aliyah out of the room. No matter what this was, as she'd told Amjad, it was far more than she'd ever dreamed of.

She was marrying Shaheen. She was having his baby.

Those were the true miracles.

Ten

Johara's tiny procession started to pick up followers as soon as they stepped out of the corridor leading from her quarters.

Each time she looked behind her, more women had joined the queue, and soon there were a few dozen of them, smiling from ear to ear and giggling in her wake.

Each group of four was dressed in the same outfit, with the colors of each group's attire a variation in deeper shades of the same cream and beige colors. By the time she looked back before they reached the main palace floor, the formation of the queue and the gradation in colors from lightest right behind her to the deepest at the end of it left her in no doubt.

They were her bridal procession.

She heard Laylah groaning. "Oh, man. I feel like a peacock!"

Aliyah looked down at her dress of deep reds and oranges. "And I feel like a fire breathing dragon. Someone should have told us what the color scheme was going to be."

"By someone," Laylah put in, in case Johara missed it, which in her condition, she *had,* "we mean your groom, who's going to pay big-time for deciding your bridal procession outfits based on the dress he picked for you, and leaving us in the dark. Or I should say, in Technicolor."

"Years from now," Aliyah groaned, "your children are going to look at your wedding album and ask you why their aunties were perched on your sides looking like parrots."

"You're actually the splash of color bringing all this to life." They both gave her yeah, *sure,* looks and she insisted, "I could never carry off those colors, and Shaheen knew it. But your brand of vivid beauty should never be subjected to anything less fiery and vital. And that is my professional opinion. I would never pick anything but bold, vibrant colors for either of you. And I can't wait to design you some outfits that only you can do justice!"

"I always thought I'd like you if I got to know you. I was wrong." Laylah hugged her exuberantly. "I'm going to *love* you."

Aliyah hugged her on the other side. "I already do. It's enough to feel how much you love Shaheen."

Johara met Aliyah's eyes and realized that was why Aliyah had decided she was innocent of stealing the jewels. As a woman in love herself, Aliyah had recognized that Johara would rather die than cause Shaheen heartache or harm.

Feeling her tears welling, she distracted herself

by focusing on her surroundings. She wasn't going to Shaheen with red eyes and streaked makeup.

Soon, the splendor she was rushing through occupied her focus for real—the palace she'd considered home, where she'd lived for most of her childhood, the best part of her life.

It was growing up here that had fanned the flames of the artistic tendencies she'd inherited from her parents. Moving from the plain practicality of New Jersey to this wonderland of embellishments and exoticness and grandeur blended from Persian, Ottoman and Mughal influences had fired her imagination from her first day here.

The palace had taken thousands of artisans and craftsmen three decades to finish in the mid-seventeenth century, and it had always felt to her as if the accumulation of history resonated in its halls, inhabited it walls. As much as the ancient bloodlines with all their trials and triumphs coursed through Shaheen's and his family's veins and stamped their bearing and characters, each inch of this place had been maintained as a testament to Zohayd's greatness and the prosperity of its ruling house.

But all that would be for nothing if the jewels were not found. If she couldn't figure out who'd forged them…

"We're here!"

"Here" was before the doors to the ceremony hall where the bridal parade had been held for Shaheen. Though it had been agony to be there that night, she'd still felt the wonder of being there again.

As a child she hadn't been allowed to attend royal functions held there. But when all was quiet, Shaheen had taken her there as frequently as she wished, to stay as long as she wanted, having the place all to herself to draw each corner of it, each inlay detail, each pierce work, each calligraphy panel.

The octagonal hall had always felt as if all the greatness, purpose and philosophy of the palace's design converged there. It was the palace hub, gracefully enclosed by its central marble one-hundred-foot wide and high dome, its walls spread with intricate, geometric shapes, its eight soaring arches defining its space at ground level, each crowned by a second arch midway up the wall with the upper arches forming balconies. It was from those that she'd learned her best lessons of drawing perspective.

A few dozen feet from the hall's soaring double doors, which were heavily worked in embossed bronze, gold and silver Zohaydan motifs, the music became louder. The quartertone-dominated Zohaydan music with its Indian, Turkish and Arabian influences and exotic instrumental arrangement and rhythm swept through the air, riding the fumes and scents of incense.

Then four footmen in black outfits embroidered with gold thread pulled back the massive doors by their circular knobs.

She stumbled to a stop, everything falling away.

She'd thought the ceremony would be a damage-control affair that would boil down to two purposes—the king's to publicize their so-called secret marriage, and theirs, to get her hands on the fake jewels. But this… this…

She hadn't, couldn't have expected *this*.

She moved again, propelled by the momentum of her companions across a threshold that felt as if it opened into another realm. Into a scene lifted right out of the most lavish of *One Thousand and One Nights*.

From every arch hung rows of incense burners and

flaming torches, against every wall rested miraculous arrangements of white and golden roses among backgrounds of lush foliage. Each pillar was wrapped in bronze satin that rained silver tassels and was worked heavily in gold patterns. Sparkling gold dust covered the marble floor. Everything shimmered under the ambient light like Midas's vault, among the swirling sweetness of *ood,* musk and amber fumes.

And studding the scene were far more than the two thousand people who'd populated the first and only ceremony she'd attended here. A mind-boggling assortment, from those dressed in the latest exclusive fashions to those who did look as if they'd just stepped out of *Arabian Nights.*

Her feverish eyes made erratic stops as she recognized faces. King Atef and King Kamal, sitting on a platform to one side on thronelike seats. Dozens of highest-order international political figures and celebrities. Queen Sondoss and Shaheen's half brothers, Haidar and Jalal, among probably every other adult Aal Shalaan and their relatives.

The only one she couldn't see was Shaheen.

Shaheen…he'd done all this. For her. But when? How? Where was he? She couldn't be here, face all this, without him…

"Johara! Breathe!"

She gulped a breath at Laylah's prodding. Then another.

"*Stop.* You've hyperventilating," Aliyah exclaimed.

She forced herself to regulate her breathing. She could just see the headlines if she fainted.

Pregnant Aal Shalaan Bride Passes Out At Wedding Ceremony.

Her vision had cleared and her steps had firmed when

the openly gawking crowd parted to stand on two sides as she and her procession made their way through. She felt she was treading the insubstantial ground of a dream as the thunder of clapping rose and the music, which she realized issued from an extensive live ensemble, began the distinctive percussive melody of the most popular Zohaydan wedding song, the one that called everyone to come wonder at the bride's splendor and her groom's phenomenal luck. By the time Aliyah and Laylah were singing along, she was floating on auto.

Then she saw her father.

He was mounting three gold-satin covered steps to a gold-satin-covered platform at the epicenter of the hall. She'd chosen him to act as her proxy, the one who would put his hand in Shaheen's during the ritual. She'd thought they'd all sit down and it would be over in minutes. Now it seemed his role included taking her to her groom with all the ceremony of this carefully choreographed piece.

She'd seen him for minutes last night with Shaheen and the king and only to tell him of the situation. To say he'd been shocked would be the understatement of the century.

He now waited for her, the litheness of his figure accentuated in a tight-fitting bronze silk tunic and pants, his chest heavy with the shining and colorful medals of honor and distinction he'd received throughout his service, his broad shoulders bearing the tags of the highest rank he'd quit. She felt Aliyah and Laylah fall behind as she climbed the steps, each diverging on one side of the platform to lead a portion of her procession to form a circle around it. As she reached the top, her father took her hands in his, his earlier shock replaced by lingering bewilderment tinged by guarded joy.

But it was the apology that lurked in the depths of his black eyes that made her pull him to her in a fierce hug.

He let out a ragged breath as his arms trembled around her. "I'm sorry I was so absorbed in my own problems I didn't notice what was going on with you. Is that why you felt you couldn't tell me? You thought I couldn't be there for you?"

Mortification rose inside her. She wasn't letting him in on more than he could think. She hugged him tighter. "*No.* If it concerns only me, I will always let you in, Daddy."

"But it concerned Shaheen, too, and you were protecting him." She nodded into his shoulder. He sighed, pulled back to look at her, his eyes level with hers. "You love him?" She nodded again, knew she didn't have to say how much or for how long. It was there in her eyes. "Then this is the best thing that ever happened to me, to see you marry the man you love. I can't think of a better man for you, or a better man, period. I do think Shaheen is the best of all the princes. And you know how highly I think of them all."

"Even me, Berj? You think highly of me?" Johara jerked as Amjad descended on her and father's tête-à-tête, clamping her father's shoulder and tugging him under his, looking down into his startled eyes, his radiating that ruthless shrewdness and uncanny emerald fire. "Now, where could I have possibly gone wrong?"

"Crown Prince Amjad…" Her father looked totally confused. "I meant no offense…"

"Oh, don't apologize to him, Dad." Johara glared up into Amjad's merciless teasing, trying to gauge if he was going to do more than tease, all but baring her teeth, warning him off.

"My impending sister-in-law has spoken." Amjad did that thing he did so well, looking one in the eye and talking about them in third person, sidelining them. "Seems you've been granted license to offend, Berj. And I hope you'll also reconsider your high opinion. We wouldn't want to give me a good name, now would we?"

As her father smiled like someone who'd just walked into the middle of a conversation and was too embarrassed to ask what it was about, Amjad's eyes traveled down the mind-boggling simulation of the pure gold cascading choker necklace, encrusted in two hundred fifty carats of diamonds ranging from pure ice to golden yellow, that covered her from high on her neck to the edge of her décolleté. "So which, in your opinion, is the *real* Pride of Zohayd, Berj? Your daughter or this?"

He touched the necklace. She stamped her foot on top of his.

Amjad didn't even wince as her high heel jammed between his bones, his only response an intensifying of the bedeviling in his eyes. The tug of war had been subtle enough to go unnoticed by all, so her father almost jerked in shock when Amjad threw his head back on a guffaw as if out of the blue. The sound was so predatory it would have scared her if she weren't so furious.

She was about to hiss to Amjad that she wasn't above making a more overt retaliation if he dared renege on their deal when a storm of murmurs mushroomed, drowning out the music and her intentions.

As the crowd turned in a wave toward the new focus of attention, she knew. It was Shaheen.

"Grandstander," Amjad murmured. Then he bent to

deliver his next words in her ears. "Enjoy. But not so much that you forget what this is all about."

"And don't *you* forget my special forces gathered right outside this hall."

Harres had materialized on her other side. He gave her a bolstering smile and Amjad a subtle tug, making him fall back, gesturing for her and Berj to precede them.

The moment their quartet descended from the other side of the platform, the lights dimmed, until the hall was dipped in darkness with only a spotlight following her procession, focused on her. She couldn't see anything beyond her next step.

Her stampeding heart shifted into higher gear. She could feel that she was moving deeper into Shaheen's orbit, felt his eyes on her, caressing her, loving her.

And though she couldn't see him, she opened herself, letting him see everything inside her. Along with all of her that he knew he had, she gave him her gratitude that he hadn't let this be a rushed apology of a ceremony. Even if she was dying of embarrassment, would have preferred something far more private and far, far less extravagant, she knew this was his way of shouting to the world his pride of being hers the loudest he could.

And she knew it was already causing untold damages.

She'd noted the pointed absence of all the tribes they'd been negotiating with. She could only surmise the worst.

But for now, he was giving her more miracles by the moment. And she would take them all and treasure each forever.

The music changed into a hotter rhythm. Her heart followed suit as the spotlight following her split in two, the duplicate inching away, leading her gaze with its sweep.

Then it fell on him.

She stopped, yanked her father to a halt with her, heard Amjad snort as he and Harres almost walked into them. But nothing mattered. Nothing but Shaheen.

It was the first time she'd seen him like this. And she'd thought he looked like a desert god in modern clothes!

Now, swathed in the trappings of his heritage, the distillation of its art and chivalry and history, he was beyond description. And his eyes were telling her he cared about only one thing. Becoming hers.

She moved again, the desire to examine his every detail more closely galvanizing her.

The vigorous waves of his hair, now brushing his collar, gleamed deepest mahogany under the spotlight, which struck tongues of flame from his fiery-brown eyes. His face had never looked more noble, more potent, with every slash of character carved deeper in the stark light. The rest of his perfection was encased in a three-piece outfit fashioned from heavy *jamawar* silk in browns and golds echoing her own clothing. A scarf printed with the royal insignia in an ingenious repetition and gathered by a dazzling brooch, another piece from the Pride of Zohayd, overlaid his high-collared, fitted golden top. A wide bronze satin sash connected the top to deeper bronze pants that stretched over the power of his thighs and legs, billowing at their ends to gather into burnt brown polished leather boots.

But it was the cloak on top of it all that that made her feel he'd come to her from a trip through the past.

The color of darkest, richest earth, it fell from his endless shoulders in relaxed pleats to his feet, looked as if it were constantly sighing in pleasure to be surrounding him. Embroidery on its front panel descended in a wide V to his waist level, the gold thread and beads forming such elaborate motifs, the artist in her salivated for the chance to examine their formation and realization. The embellishments seemed to accentuate his masculinity, if that was possible.

With her every step nearer, he tensed, and the cloak seemed to bate its breath with him for her arrival. She wished he'd hide her within it, transport her away from all the pomp and attention.

But she knew he was doing this for her, to honor her, to show her that this was no damage-control maneuver but the one thing he wanted to do, was proud to, and was doing with as much fanfare as possible so no one would mistake his desire and pride.

Before she could throw herself into his arms, a blonde woman in a cream sarilike outfit and a man as tall as Shaheen in all-black with midnight hair down to his shoulders stepped out of the darkness into the circle of light.

Johara almost choked.

She'd been sad that this would be too rushed, too hushed, not even a real wedding, that she wouldn't have them here. But Shaheen…he…he…

He'd brought her mother and brother to her!

For a stunned moment, her mind compensated for her body's inability to move, streaked.

She hadn't seen Aram face-to-face in over a year. She'd missed him terribly, drank in the sight of him now. He looked more like a pirate than ever, seeming to grow more imposing with each passing year, her total opposite in coloring, having inherited her mother's dazzling turquoise eyes and their father's swarthy complexion and night-black hair, and combining their mother's family's height with the sturdiness and breadth of their father's. Her mother looked her eternally beautiful self.

And she surged to them, encompassed them with Shaheen in her delight. Her kisses moved from her mother to Aram, ended all over Shaheen's face with a reiteration of thanks, for this gift, his best yet.

The music changed yet again, to take on a more solemn and momentous timber, to herald the next stage in the ceremony.

Her mother caught her closer, kissed her again. "*Ma cherie,* I never thought this day would come to pass. I was so worried about you."

Johara pulled back from her, stunned. "You knew?"

"I always knew." Her mother's eyes grew more brilliant with tears. "It's why I never wanted to come back here. I didn't want you exposed to heartache. I thought your love for Shaheen would only hurt you, since it was impossible. I can't tell you how relieved I am, how happy that I was wrong."

She surrendered to her mother's fierce hug again, processing this new knowledge. Seemed she was totally useless in keeping a secret. Everyone except her father had read her like an open book.

Then a thought struck her and she pushed out of her mother's arms and rounded on Aram. "Which reminds me!" She glowered her displeasure at him. "*You* were wrong."

He looked taken aback for a second, his eyes flying accusingly to Shaheen, before he looked back at her, smirking. "If this doesn't prove I was right, I don't know what does."

"You were wrong *then.* And I want an apology!"

"I won't apologize for doing what I had to, to protect you."

"Oh, you *will* apologize. To Shaheen! How could you accuse him of…any of that? You of all people, his *supposed* best friend?"

"You're not going to have *another* sibling fight right here, are you?" Harres groaned. "I thought we've had enough of those."

"No such thing as enough sibling fights," Amjad said, his very voice an incitement. "And again, when better? I say this is long overdue. Have at it, boys and girls."

Aram bared his teeth. "I didn't realize how much I missed you, Amjad."

Amjad grinned back, baring the demon inhabiting his own body. "Was that my cue to say I missed you, too? Oops, missed it."

Johara's father cleared his throat. "I'm realizing with each passing second that I know nothing about what's been going on around me, but will you take pity on me and not make me feel more like the deaf in the parade here?"

Johara and Aram hugged him in apology. Shaheen let it last a moment, then he put his arms around the quartet of her family.

"There will be no more fights among us." He looked emphatically among them. He meant all of them. Him and Aram, her and Aram, her mother and father. He didn't continue until he got their consenting nods. "Now we need to put the *ma'zoon* out of his misery. After he finishes marrying us, he will spend the rest of the night printing our royal book of matrimony."

With that, they broke apart, and her father placed her hand in Shaheen's. Shaheen hugged her to his side as he led her and their procession to their final destination, a gilded woodwork miniature of the palace—the *kousha*—where the *ma'zoon* awaited them, and where they'd sit throughout the wedding proceedings.

As they sat down on the silk brocade couch, Johara between Shaheen and her father and the rest of their family on either side, she exchanged a look of total love and alliance with him.

Then the ritual began.

Three hours of escalating festivities later, Johara stood jangling in the aftermath of it all in Shaheen's bedroom, at his dresser, taking off the jewels.

He'd told her he'd wanted to take her to their home by the sea, or even fly them away and have their wedding night on board his jet. But the jewels were prohibited from leaving the palace.

She was completely okay with it. She'd been imagining being with him in this room ever since their aborted time together the night he'd come back to Zohayd.

He'd gone to inform their fathers that the jewels would be returned in the morning. When she asked what excuse he'd given for that, he made her wish she hadn't. She blushed now thinking about it.

"Take your *dupatta* off, *ya joharti.*"

She spun around as the hunger in his bass rumble licked her back. She watched as he approached, her hands automatically rising to obey him.

As her *dupatta* slid off her head, he snapped his scarf off his neck, hurled it to the floor. "Now your *lehenga.*"

She obeyed again, at once, unable to wait to be free

of her clothes and crushed beneath him, taken, invaded, made whole.

He covered more of the two dozen feet between them, giving up his cloak for her skirt, then his top for hers. She swallowed over and over at the sight as each move gave her a show of rippling strength and symmetry. Soon all that remained were her panties, and she gave him those for his sash. All she had left on were her three-inch sandals.

"This is the ultimate unfairness," she croaked as he stopped before her in his low-riding pants and boots, a colossus carved by gods of virility. "You always have more clothes."

His eyes crinkled as they swept over her, the fire in them rising, singeing her. "I wish I can take credit for that. There's no higher cause than feasting on your nakedness."

"You can take credit this time." She cupped her breasts, trying to assuage their aching. "For everything. Today was beyond anything I ever dreamed of, *ya habibi.* The outfit, the thought behind it, the note, every last detail of this night, Mom and Aram. I have no words to tell you what your thoughtfulness meant to me. What *you* mean to me. You've always meant…everything. Now…now… No…there are no words. I only hope you'll always let me show you how much I love you, as you keep showing me."

She trembled with the magnitude of her love and gratitude, that he existed, that he was now hers, no matter how fleetingly. She'd loved him with everything in her from the moment he'd touched her. She'd wanted him even more when she'd felt his baby growing inside her. And now he was her husband. Her *husband.*

The knowledge made it all deeper, all-encompassing, turning her hunger for him almost into distress.

Then he put what she felt into words and made it much worse, and infinitely better. "Anything I can think of to show you my love, prove your ownership of me, will never be enough. I thought I wanted you as much as I possibly could before. But now, knowing our baby is growing inside you, knowing you're my *wife*...my desire for you makes my former ferocity seem tame and my worry of losing control an easily curbed impulse. My mind is shooting to all kinds of fanciful fears, that our union this time, with us feeling this way, might take us all the way to the edge of survival."

"So what?"

Her reckless challenge cracked his control. He dragged her by the hand, slammed her against him, breast to thigh. "So what indeed. How about we see what the edge of survival feels like?"

"Oh, yes. Yes, take me there, Shaheen, and beyond." She slithered from his hold onto her knees before him, her hands worshipping his hardness through his pants, shaking on his zipper.

As she slid it down he whipped one hand to his back, snapped something from the band of his pants before they fell to mid-thigh, allowing him to spring free, thick and daunting, dark and glistening with craving, throbbing with control.

She'd barely taken him into her mouth, licking the addictive taste of his desire from his silk-smooth crown when he pulled her up, gathering her from the ground in one arm. She cried her protest and he growled as he saluted each of her nipples with a devouring suckle. She cried out again as another wave of arousal crashed through her, her core pouring its demand for his invasion.

"You always say it's punishment, not reward, giving you pleasure without giving you me." He pressed her to the capitoné wall beside his bed. "Tonight you get reward first, then punishment later."

He made a lightning-fast move with his left hand as his right one secured her against the wall, his bulk opening her around him. She felt a sharp tug, heard a sharper click.

She tried to turn her head, to investigate, but his eyes caught hers, and everything ceased to matter, to exist.

Lava simmered in his eyes and from the erection that found her entrance. His hiss felt even hotter. "I want to invade you, finish you, perish inside you."

"Then do it, finish us both...*please...*"

He rammed into her. All his power and love and hunger behind the thrust. He slid against all the right places, places he'd created inside her, abrading nerves into an agony of response, stimulating receptors for all the sensations they could transmit. Then he moved as hard and fast as she was dying for him to.

Almost too soon she started shaking, arched against him in a deep bow, hovering at the edge of a paroxysm as the world diffused, only his beloved face in focus, clenched in pleasure, his eyes vehement with his greed for hers.

She tried to bring both arms around him to hold him as she gave everything to him, but her right hand snagged, wrenched back.

She looked down in her haze, found it shackled to his left one in a gilded handcuff.

Just the idea—that he'd done this, bound her to himself, thought of it, wanted to show her how inseparable he wanted them to be, how mind-blowingly deep, how decadently *wicked* it all was… Her senses went haywire, sent overload shearing through her.

"I did tell you I'd tie you to my wrist, didn't I?" he growled as he gave her his fiercest thrust yet and her body all but exploded in the most powerful climax he'd ever given her.

Her shriek of his name came in bursts as the convulsions of release ripped through her. Discharge after discharge of pleasure pummeled her, squeezing all of her muscles, inside and out over every part of him, his heat and weight bearing down on her and within her in waves, stimulating her to her limits and beyond.

She raved, begged. "Can't…can't…please…you…you…"

And he gave her what she needed. The sight of his face, the feel of him succumbing to the ecstasy she gave him, the pulse of his own climax inside her. They hit her at her peak, had her thrashing, weeping, unable to endure the spike in pleasure. Everything blipped, faded…

Heavy breathing and sluggish heartbeats seemed to echo from the end of a long tunnel as the scent of sex and satisfaction flooded her lungs. Awareness trickled into her body, a mess of tremors so sated she was practically numb. She felt one thing. Shaheen. Still inside her.

She opened lids weighing a ton each, saw him swim in and out of focus. She was on her back on the bed, with him kneeling between her legs, her hips on his thighs, his free palm kneading her breasts, gliding over her shoulders, her arms, her belly.

She watched him watch her, her position the image of wantonness, of surrender and trust, her free arm thrown above her head, her back arched, breasts jutting, legs opened over his hips, his shaft half-buried inside her, stretching her glistening entrance, wrapped around him in the most intimate kiss.

"So how did you like your…reward?"

"You were right…" she slurred at his deepening occupation. "This was…the edge of survival. I felt… my every cell…burst."

He set his teeth as he rocked another inch inside her. "See why I always insist on taking the edge off?" He rose off the bed, scooped her up with him, his smile all satisfaction and indulgence. "But now that I have, I can really turn to your punishment."

And for the rest of the night, among a few more rewards, he punished her with escalating inventiveness. And in continued captivity.

Johara jumped when something dropped into her lap.

She looked down and saw the handcuffs at the same moment she felt Shaheen surrounding her.

She'd been so absorbed that she hadn't felt his approach for the first time ever.

"The best morning in history to you, my crafty Gemma."

She beamed up at him, opened her mouth for his luxuriant invasion. She'd undone the handcuffs and slipped out of bed two hours ago. She couldn't bring herself to wake him up, but had been burning to examine the jewels. And she had.

He let her surface from his kiss, slid a loving touch down her cheek. "I see you've filled a whole notebook with observations. Can I hope that you have a list for us?"

"No." She saw dismay gather in his eyes and rushed to deliver the rest of her verdict. "I have better than that. I know exactly who forged these jewels."

Eleven

"Are you sure about this, *ya joharti?*"

Johara turned her eyes away from the streets of Geneva zooming by the window of their car. She'd been looking blindly outside since they'd left the airport. Shaheen's worried gaze had been touching her ever since. Now that he'd voiced his concern, she could no longer look away.

She met his solicitude and again wanted to tell him that she wasn't sure. And again dismissed the thought as it formed.

She nodded to him, kissed the hand that swept down her cheek. His eyes softened even more before they snapped back to the road.

They'd flown here on his private jet hours after she'd delivered her verdict. Not that he was asking her if she was sure of *that.* Shaheen, as she became more certain with each passing moment, took everything she said as incontrovertible fact. He had absolute faith not only in her integrity but also in her expertise. He was confident that her deduction of the identity of the forger was incontestable. Equally because he believed she knew her business, and that she wouldn't accuse someone if she wasn't certain beyond a shadow of doubt.

She was. Although she'd been tempted to say she wasn't. Because she felt the moment her role in uncovering the conspiracy was over, her time with Shaheen would be over, too.

Nothing worked to allay that fear. Not even when he said they had time to abort the conspiracy and had forever together. In fact, the more he said that, the more desperate she became. All this bliss couldn't possibly continue. Not at anything less than a terrible price. One she would be unable to let Shaheen or Zohayd pay.

She'd started counting down her remaining time with him from the moment she'd given him her verdict.

He and Harres and Amjad had at first said they'd handle it. They would besiege the forger with their special influence and force a confession. She'd insisted on being the one to approach him. She believed no coercion would be needed. Shaheen had at once trusted her judgment, supported her decision.

But he sensed her agitation, was worried that she was outside her comfort zone. And she was, if not for the reason he thought.

They stopped at a gated parking lot. The attendant recognized both of them and at once let them into the area reserved for the exclusive establishment's most elite clientele.

Shaheen stopped the car, turned to her. *"Kolloh zain?"*

She pulled him to her for a brief, fierce kiss. "Yes, everything's all right. Let's do this."

In moments they were walking hand in hand into the avant garde reception area of the showroom of LaSalle, one of the most celebrated designers of original jewelry in the world.

As more people recognized them, they were given the treatment only a star fashion designer and a billionaire prince could be given. In seconds they were let into the sanctum of Théodore LaSalle, the establishment's owner and the brand's namesake.

Dressed in fifties-movie-star elegance, the David Niven look-alike rushed to meet them in the foyer leading to his office, his face split into a wide smile of someone expecting an unrepeatable honor and a transaction worth a year of magnificent sales.

"Doesn't look as if he suspects why we're here," Shaheen muttered under his breath as the man ushered them into his office and rushed to his desk. "Or he's a superlative actor."

"What can I offer you, *mes cheries?*" LaSalle asked, one finger on his intercom. "All refreshments are available."

"That won't be necessary, *Monsieur* LaSalle," Johara said. "Please, come sit with us. We have something of extreme importance to discuss with you."

LaSalle's face fell as he walked to his sitting area, where Shaheen had led her to a love seat opposite the seat he gestured for the man to take.

Trepidation seized LaSalle's face. Shaheen said something to her in Arabic. That this looked like a guilty man. She squeezed his hand, and he nodded. Whatever he thought, he would let her deal with LaSalle. She'd told him she believed not only in the man's artistry but in his integrity, too. She would give him every benefit of the doubt first.

She started, careful not to make her words either a question or an accusation. "It's about the duplicates of the Pride of Zohayd collection, Monsieur LaSalle."

The man didn't even look at her, his gaze pinned nervously on Shaheen. Johara could imagine how her husband looked to the man, a lethal predator crouched in deceptive calm, but clearly only on a tight leash, and would launch into a slashing attack at a word from her.

"Are there any complaints about any of the pieces, Prince Aal Shalaan? I am, of course, willing to replace any that have been damaged, even if due to negligence. I produce my pieces with a lifetime guarantee. But if this is about the quality, in my defense—" he swung his gaze to her, as if asking her support "—you of all people, Mademoiselle Nazaryan—*pardonnez moi,* Princess Aal Shalaan—know the difficulty of working from photographs, even the most detailed and multiangled of close-ups."

Johara sat forward, placed a placating hand on the man's trembling one. "The quality is what only you can achieve, Monsieur. It was the sheer genius of the duplication that narrowed down my options to you. It's imperative that you tell us everything about how you came to make those duplicates."

"You mean you don't *know?*" LaSalle gaped at her. "But it was the royal house who commissioned the duplicates."

After a stunned moment when Johara thought they'd gotten this all wrong, she asked slowly, "You mean King Atef personally commissioned them?"

The man shook his expressive hands. "Of course not. I don't even know who did, but it was understood it was the royal house."

"How was it understood?" Shaheen grated.

The man gave a helpless, eloquent shrug. "Owners of invaluable treasures frequently wish to have duplicates to use if their jewelry will be worn or displayed in less than totally secure conditions."

"So who approached you from the royal house?" Shaheen asked.

"I wasn't approached directly. In fact, it was through a quite convoluted method of double blinds."

"And you still thought this was aboveboard?" Shaheen hissed.

The man was looking more mortified by the moment. "Yes. The rich and royal always wish to hide their true dealings, and it made sense that the royal house would not want it to be known that the duplicates existed. And then, who else could have provided me with all those photographs? Who could afford to pay the astronomical fee I was given?"

"Who indeed." Shaheen huffed. "But didn't it seem suspicious that they didn't entrust their own royal jeweler with the chore?"

The man nodded vigorously. "But I was told Berj was not well, and I even called him to make sure of that. My contacts said they didn't want to burden him in his state. They also feared if he heard a whiff of this, he'd feel slighted that he'd been bypassed for this assignment, that he'd feel his usefulness to the royal house had come to an end. As a fellow master craftsman, this was even more incentive for me to keep silent than the money I was paid. I appreciated my clients' need for absolute accuracy more when it was their effort not to tip him off to the fact that he'd be maintaining duplicates. I did warn them that he would know, no matter how accurate the replicas, but I was assured he was in no condition to notice, if I made them close enough."

She stared at LaSalle, a terrible suspicion spreading through her. She turned to Shaheen only to see it reflected in his eyes.

Then he put it into words. "They were certain of his inability to recognize the fakes because they've been drugging him. This explains his deteriorating condition of late. And when he believed there was something wrong with him and started taking medication for his so-called depression, the drug interactions must have caused his heart attack."

"They could have killed him!" Johara cried out, her heart rattling with rage.

Shaheen gave a solemn nod, eloquent with his determination to punish those responsible for this most of all. "But since they didn't want a new jeweler, a younger and more vigilant one in his place, they pulled back, counted on his unwarranted medications to confuse him enough for their purposes."

"This is appalling!" Monsieur LaSalle exclaimed, horror seizing his face. "I've been party not only to a fraud, but to almost having a hand in Berj's death?"

"You are not in any way accountable," Shaheen assured him. "But we need you to tell us every detail about how you were contacted, how you were paid and how you delivered the duplicates. Any information you give us will be the only leads we have toward apprehending the culprits and returning the real jewels."

The man exploded to his feet. "You have my full cooperation. And if they approach me again, I will keep playing the game, so they'll either give me more information or grow secure and do something that will help you expose them."

After they'd obtained every possible detail from LaSalle, Johara and Shaheen drove straight back to the airport.

As they approached Shaheen's jet, she saw a black Jaguar parked near its stairs. Amjad and Harres were leaning against it.

As soon as she and Shaheen stepped out of the car, Harres met them. Amjad remained where he was, hips braced against the hood, legs crossed at the ankles and hands deep in his pockets.

"Any news?" Harres asked.

"What we can use only, please," Amjad interjected.

Shaheen shot him an exasperated glance then answered Harres. "The forger is a reputable jeweler who was duped like the rest of us. He offered to do all he can and promised to keep working with us."

Amjad sighed. "If you say so. Or is it Johara who does?"

Shaheen ignored him. "The thieves have access to funds on par with us. And they have infiltrated the palace on every level." He gave Harres the tape with LaSalle's recorded details. "I think this has enough threads to lead us to the mastermind."

Harres put the tape in his pocket. "I've already started investigating everyone who was in the palace during the past year. But this will narrow down my search. It will narrow down your sweep, too, Amjad."

Amjad shrugged, the picture of nonchalance. "Why should I narrow it down? I'm having a ball tracing every transaction that occurred in the accounts of everyone who was *ever* in the palace and cross-referencing those with just about everyone in the region and their dogs. Even after I find the funds exchanged in the conspiracy and the hands that exchanged them, I'm keeping this up. Seems the Pride of Zohayd is not the only treasure to be found here. I'm exposing dozens of priceless secrets. I now have something ruinous on just about everyone, it's just sublime."

Harres thumped Amjad on the back. "What he meant by all that is that he, like all of us, is forever in your debt, Johara."

Johara looked Amjad in the eye. "I'll accept his gratitude when he actually proves effective in getting the jewels back."

Amjad's lethal smile acknowledged her third-person payback. "Oh, I will. But now it's time to return to Zohayd and face the music. Harres should have stayed back and announced code red. Your wedding has the tribes up in arms. Expect the worst."

The moment they touched down in Zohayd, the king summoned them. And it was clear the worst *was* to be expected.

It still took hearing it to make it real, to tip her from the edge and into the nightmare.

"The council is in session right now, Shaheen," King Atef said as soon as they entered his stateroom, his voice heavy with sorrow. "They have made a final decree. You are to dissolve your marriage to Johara. A bride has been unanimously chosen for you, and neither she nor her family will accept her being a second wife. And they demand that her offspring be your heir, not your child from Johara. They are gathering their people on our borders, in all the hubs of unrest within the kingdom. They say your answer would decide their next actions."

Johara felt as if a scythe had cut her down at the knees. Shaheen's arm came around her, held her up, hugged to him.

"Don't worry about those thugs, Father," Harres growled. "I'll send them running with their tails between their legs."

"And afterward, Harres?" Everyone, including Harres was startled when Shaheen spoke up. Johara shuddered at his calmness. "You think force will create any long-term or real peace?"

Harres's scowl was spectacular. She could see him fighting to the death over this. "They're bluffing, and I'll show them that I don't take kindly to bluffs. And if they're not, I'll show them I'm even less forgiving of threats. This same council entrusted me with the peacekeeping of this kingdom, and *B'Ellahi,* I'm keeping it."

"This is not a bluff, Harres," King Atef said. "And if they carry out their threats, it is my fault. I've misled them for too long. Now they're enraged. And unreasonable."

Aggression blazed in Harres's feral eyes. "Give me the word, and I'll show them unreasonable!"

Amjad stayed pointedly silent through it all. Watching her.

Shaheen only shook his head at Harres. "There will be no need for any of that." He turned to his father. "I wish you'd let them tell me that to my face instead of hiding behind you and burdening you with their pompous and insane demands." Then he turned to her. "Stay here, *ya galbi*. I'll be back in minutes."

Johara watched Shaheen walk away and felt as if she'd lost him already. He would try to talk the council out of their decision. And he'd fail.

Her vision swam as it wavered to the men who'd been a major part of her life. They were Shaheen's family, were hers, too. Harres growled that he'd beat back any attempt at an uprising so hard, the dead would reconsider their mutinies. The king argued that he couldn't give the order to plunge the kingdom into war. Amjad watched her. She sank deeper in despair.

Then Shaheen came back. His *kabeer el yaweran* was behind him, laden in dossiers.

He took her hand to his lips then folded her arm through the crook of his. "Shall we, *ya joharet galbi?*"

She walked only because he steered her, could barely see the route they took through the palace to the council hall or the Roman senatelike assembly all around them once they entered it, barely heard the din die down as Shaheen brought her to a stop in the middle of the floor.

He spoke at once, his voice an awe-striking boom. "I will never divorce Johara. Or take a second wife. And this is final."

The hall exploded.

Shaheen raised his voice over the cacophony. "But…I have a solution."

The clamor again died down as everyone recognized the determination and certainty in Shaheen's voice and demeanor.

He went on once there was total silence. "My solution will exonerate my king, my family and my tribe of my actions, end any ill will you now bear toward them."

He let a beat pass when everyone and everything seemed to hold their breath. Then he said, "Exile me."

Johara's heart stopped.

She felt every heart in the gigantic hall follow suit.

Then Shaheen continued, and her heart burst into thundering shock and horror. "I offer that my family disown me, strip me of my name, and for the kingdom of Zohayd to forever forbid me, and my children, entry to its soil."

As the uproar rose again, his voice again drowned it out. "But this will only appease the insult I've dealt you by breaking my vows. To compensate you, my venerable lords, for any loss you may suffer from my refusal to enter the beneficial union you demanded…" He beckoned for his *kabeer el yaweran* to come forward. "I give you all my assets."

Silence crashed over the hall.

Nothingness roared inside Johara.

Shaheen was saying…offering…

Suddenly, a voice rent the silence. "Yes, make an example of Shaheen Aal Shalaan!"

Another roared, "It's the only way to appease our tribes. Exile him!"

More voices rose, tangled.

"Prove that not even the king's son can renege on his word."

"Show every royal they cannot play with us all and get away with it."

Shaheen only smiled down at her. The smile of someone who'd achieved exactly what he was after. Then he steered her away and out of the council hall.

They might have walked two steps or two miles when it all sank in. She wrenched on his hand, bringing him to a stop.

"Are you out of your *mind?*"

His smile broadened, his face the picture of relief. "I've never been more in it, and I—"

She cut him off, words colliding as they spilled out of her. "*This* is what you meant every time you told me you'll resolve this? *This* was your solution all along?"

"Yes. It took me a while to work out the details that will hand everything I own and control over to others without causing the businesses to collapse or the people populating them to go bankrupt or lose their jobs—"

She barged in on his explanation, panting now, almost raving. "But that is not a solution! That…this…is a *catastrophe.* You're sacrificing everything that you *are!*"

"And I'm so relieved this is over. It's *not* a sacrifice, by the way, just a tiny price to have you and our baby. But you don't have to worry. I'll rebuild my success and my fortune."

"I'm not worried about *that.*" She stamped her foot, feeling her brain overheating, her body shaking apart. "I'm making more money all the time and I have enough for both of us, which you can use as capital to rebuild your empire. What I am is *devastated* at the enormity of the sacrifices you just offered—your name, your family, your country, everything you've worked for…"

And he dared chuckle. "So what? I have a wife who'll support me."

She gave a chagrined shriek. "You…you…" Words shriveled to ashes in her mouth. Only one hope remained. "They'll say no."

"Oh, no, they won't. If we'd stayed one more minute, we'd have been flooded in the drool of their eagerness to grab my assets. I'm worth far more to them dead and gone, figuratively speaking, than alive and begetting children of their blood."

And she grabbed him by the arms and shook him. "Go back right now and say you take it all back! You tell them that you—"

He hugged her off the ground, ending her tirade. Before she could twist out of his arms, he buried his face in her neck. "I'm not repeating my father's mistakes, *ya galbi.* He gave up his only chance at love, married women he could barely tolerate for the sake of his kingdom and throne. But I'm giving away replaceable things, just giving the tribes what they want so I can be what I want to be. Yours. It doesn't matter what else I am." She squirmed in his arms, sobbed, and he only pressed her closer. "I'll always remain who I am, in my heart, to my loved ones. As for my success, it might have been in part due to my status before, but now I am formidable in my own right with my knowledge and experience. Even if I never attain the same success or wealth again, what does it matter when I have the ultimate treasure—you and our baby?"

She at last made him put some distance between them, took his face in her trembling hands. "But you'll *always* have us, no price needed. Divorce me, Shaheen, give them the marriage they want. Both I and our baby will be yours forever, no matter what."

"Okay, Romeo and Juliet, move it."

Johara jerked as a hand clamped her arm. It was Amjad. He was also holding Shaheen's arm. Before either of them could say anything, he dragged them back into the council hall.

In the middle of the floor where they'd stood minutes ago, he stopped and stepped in front of them.

"All right, *venerable* lords, listen carefully." The noise again dissipated at Amjad's terrifying growl. "You always called me the Mad Prince, and now's your chance to find out just how crazy I am. All you have to do is vote against Shaheen, and I'll make each and every one of you and your spawn into the next five generations sorry to have ever been born."

"I second that." Harres came forward to stand beside Amjad.

Shaheen's younger half brothers, Haidar and Jalal, joined the lineup, forming a barricade of towering manhood and power in front of her and Shaheen.

"Third and fourth, here," Haidar said for both him and his twin. "You might be all-powerful tribal lords here, but let us remind you *we* are not just the king's sons. Each of us packs more power in the world at large than you can probably imagine."

"You *don't* want to make enemies of us." Jalal's face was reminiscent of Amjad's cruel handsomeness, a younger and even more reckless version of Amjad's demon evidently incubating inside him.

Harres gave his younger brothers a look of approval. "So to sum up, if you vote to exile Shaheen, if you touch a cent of his assets, we will all be your enemies until the day you die."

"*But,* if you free him and apologize for all you've put him through," Haidar elaborated, "you'll have our… gratitude."

Amjad gave a loud, irreverent snort. "Yeah. And you do want to see me grateful, I assure you. You will love it."

Harres nodded. "So either join us in the twenty-first

century, forget the blood-mixing rituals and do business through more…lucrative means, or…piss us off. Your choice."

With that, the brothers turned and started to walk out.

Shaheen pushed at them. "I *won't* let you do this—"

Amjad grabbed Shaheen's arm, dragged him along, hissing, "Ever heard of a strategic withdrawal, Romeo? Walk with me."

Once outside, Amjad flicked a hand at the guards and they all scattered. Then he hooked his hands low on his powerful hips, twisting his lips at Shaheen. "What's wrong with you? We were driving a bargain in there. You don't outbid your team."

Harres gave a harsh laugh. "And the greedy blowhards are having mini heart attacks in there, thinking of all they could milk out of our carte blanche."

Shaheen shook his head, adamant. "I won't let you do this. This is my responsibility."

Amjad rolled his eyes. "Bored now."

Harres turned to Haidar and Jalal, sent them back into the hall to find out the council's verdict.

Once they left, Johara realized he'd sent his younger brothers away so that he could talk freely. "I only wish we could tell the council they actually *owe* you, and more so Johara, more than they could ever repay, for giving us the first solid leads to abort the conspiracy that would tear apart the kingdom they're squabbling over pieces of."

Haidar and Jalal came back almost as soon as they'd gone in, their faces spread with cynical smiles.

"That had to be the fastest decision in the history of the kingdom," Jalal chuckled. "Money sure talks, and talks big."

Amjad slapped him on the back. "Shut up and spit it out."

Jalal smirked at him. "They release Shaheen of his vows, demand no punishment. And to 'give peace a chance,' they're 'willing' to negotiate a 'suitable' compensation."

Johara shook with relief and confusion, still unsure what this meant for all of them, what kind of losses they'd sustain so she and Shaheen could remain together.

"That's it?" She heard her voice trembling on the question. "They want…money? Why didn't they just ask for it in the first place?"

Shaheen put a finger below her chin, raised her face to his, his eyes adoring. "You would have ransomed me, *ya joharti?*"

She gave a vigorous nod. "I certainly would have. I will pay all I have now as part of this compensation."

Shaheen hugged her closer, delighted, defusing her turmoil. "They wouldn't have taken anything in settlement without reaching this point of crisis. The ways of tradition are too demanding, and people in our region have entered grueling and needless wars to keep a vow or save face." He turned to his brothers. "I know they wouldn't have agreed no matter how much they had to gain if you hadn't stood together and scared them off. You have my and Johara's gratitude, but now that they've given up the macho posturing, I'll be the one to negotiate with them. Money, as Jalal said, and massive favors are more potent than magic."

"And let you give up your right as the 'middle' child to always cause us the most trouble?" Jalal winked at him.

"It is more cost effective to give those vultures bites of each of us rather than help you rebuild your empire." Haidar grabbed Jalal and turned back to the hall. "Now excuse us as we get to the nitty gritty on the bite sizes expected."

Shaheen called out after them, "If I'd let those vultures pick apart said empire, I wouldn't have needed your help. I have a standing offer from my princess to bail me out of anything."

Johara heard their laughter until they disappeared.

Then Shaheen turned to Amjad and Harres. "Before they come back again, let's get this out of the way. Now, I'll take care of our so-called allies, while you root out our hidden enemies."

Amjad patted him on the back, all condescension. "Yeah, you two run along now and leave this to the grown-ups."

Shaheen grinned at him, then turned to exchange some last details with Harres.

Johara put her hand on Amjad's arm. "You helped Shaheen and I stay together, at a great price to yourself. Is that your way of 'atoning'? Of saying you're taking back everything you said about me?"

Amjad's eyes looked even more ruthless for their mock chagrin. "How can I possibly do that? You're a woman, aren't you?"

"Your mother was a woman."

Amjad cracked a guffaw. "And you've just made my case."

"What about your aunt? Your sister and cousin?"

Amjad made a simulation of being deep in thought. "There *might* be some anomalies in the species."

"Any hope I fall into the same anomalous category?"

"Could be." Amjad's eyes grew pondering, penetrating. "I'll reserve my final verdict. For a couple of… decades."

"Don't listen to this doomsayer, Johara." Harres put his arm around her shoulder. "You're our Johara and we all love you."

Amjad gave him an abrasive look. "And some of us would not only die for you, they were about to delete themselves from existence for you, too." His gaze moved to Shaheen. "Idiot."

Shaheen threw his head back on an exhilarated laugh. "And I can't wait for the day a woman comes along and makes you wish to delete yourself for her."

"She already came along. And almost did the job herself."

Johara's heart convulsed. The sarcasm in Amjad's voice only made her see how deep the scar went. All the way through him. She was mortified to remember how she'd accused him of being unable to love. What if this wasn't only betrayal and anger, but mortally wounded love, too?

Then Amjad opened his mouth and snuffed any compassion. "So we're off to see about our enemies, and you sleep lightly next to your bride. Now that you're all hers with a cherry on top, she might kill you—with too much love."

Harres guffawed. "One day, Amjad, a woman will make you beg her to kill you the same way. She's out there for you."

Amjad gave him one of those demolishing looks she was sure would disintegrate others. "Says the man who's gone through every unattached woman in the northern hemisphere from the age of twenty-five to forty and hasn't found 'the one' for him yet."

"I'll leave you to debate the existence of women for either of you. I'm taking the one I was born to love—" Shaheen paused for Amjad to oblige him with a snort

"—to have our honeymoon, away from all snorters and conspirators."

With one last thankful glance at them, one she shared, he swept her up in his arms.

Ecstatic, overcome, she buried her face in his neck, her heart too full to do anything but murmur her love over and over.

A long time later, entangled in the luxury of their intimacy with the sea breeze caressing their cooling bodies, Shaheen rose on his elbow beside her.

He ran his hand lovingly over her still flat belly. "You know, I'm only sorry my plan didn't work. If they'd exiled me, I would have proved to you that you *are* far more precious than everything I am or have, than life itself. But I have the rest of my life to prove this to you."

"You already did. You do, with every breath." She caressed his beloved face, bliss running down her cheeks. "And I'll spend my life proving to you that you are as precious to me."

He hugged her to him. "You already did, the day you let go and trusted me to catch you. How many times have you trusted me since? With your heart, your body, your happiness, your future? And your helping us expose the conspiracy when you know whoever is plotting it will do anything to keep it hushed, putting yourself on the line with us."

"We're in this together, all of it, for better or for worse." She kissed him with all the fierceness of her love, the profundity of her pledge. "Thank you, *ya habibi,* for saving me, for loving me, for existing and being everything to me."

He drowned her in another kiss before he pulled back.

"And I have one more thing I haven't thanked *you* for yet."

She gazed up at him, awash in love and ecstasy, waited for him to tell her one more thing that would hone the perfection.

And he did. "Thank you for never forgetting me, for seeking me out again, and giving me my life's reason. You, and our baby."

* * * * *

Much more is in store for the powerful
Aal Shalaan brothers!
Look for Olivia Gates's next Pride of Zohayd book
TO TEMPT A SHEIKH
Coming in February 2011.
Only from Silhouette Desire!

Silhouette® Desire

COMING NEXT MONTH

Available December 7, 2010

#2053 THE TYCOON'S PATERNITY AGENDA
Michelle Celmer
Man of the Month

#2054 WILL OF STEEL
Diana Palmer
The Men of Medicine Ridge

#2055 INHERITING HIS SECRET CHRISTMAS BABY
Heidi Betts
Dynasties: The Jarrods

#2056 UNDER THE MILLIONAIRE'S MISTLETOE
"The Wrong Brother"—Maureen Child
"Mistletoe Magic"—Sandra Hyatt

#2057 DANTE'S MARRIAGE PACT
Day Leclaire
The Dante Legacy

#2058 SWEET SURRENDER, BABY SURPRISE
Kate Carlisle

SDCNM1110

REQUEST YOUR FREE BOOKS!

2 FREE NOVELS PLUS 2 FREE GIFTS!

Silhouette® Desire®

Passionate, Powerful, Provocative!

YES! Please send me 2 FREE Silhouette Desire® novels and my 2 FREE gifts (gifts are worth about $10). After receiving them, if I don't wish to receive any more books, I can return the shipping statement marked "cancel." If I don't cancel, I will receive 6 brand-new novels every month and be billed just $4.05 per book in the U.S. or $4.74 per book in Canada. That's a saving of at least 15% off the cover price! It's quite a bargain! Shipping and handling is just 50¢ per book.* I understand that accepting the 2 free books and gifts places me under no obligation to buy anything. I can always return a shipment and cancel at any time. Even if I never buy another book, the two free books and gifts are mine to keep forever.

225/326 SDN E5QG

Name (PLEASE PRINT)

Address Apt. #

City State/Prov. Zip/Postal Code

Signature (if under 18, a parent or guardian must sign)

Mail to the **Silhouette Reader Service:**

IN U.S.A.: P.O. Box 1867, Buffalo, NY 14240-1867
IN CANADA: P.O. Box 609, Fort Erie, Ontario L2A 5X3

Not valid for current subscribers to Silhouette Desire books.

Want to try two free books from another line?
Call 1-800-873-8635 or visit www.morefreebooks.com.

* Terms and prices subject to change without notice. Prices do not include applicable taxes. N.Y. residents add applicable sales tax. Canadian residents will be charged applicable provincial taxes and GST. Offer not valid in Quebec. This offer is limited to one order per household. All orders subject to approval. Credit or debit balances in a customer's account(s) may be offset by any other outstanding balance owed by or to the customer. Please allow 4 to 6 weeks for delivery. Offer available while quantities last.

Your Privacy: Silhouette Books is committed to protecting your privacy. Our Privacy Policy is available online at www.eHarlequin.com or upon request from the Reader Service. From time to time we make our lists of customers available to reputable third parties who may have a product or service of interest to you. If you would prefer we not share your name and address, please check here. ☐

Help us get it right—We strive for accurate, respectful and relevant communications. To clarify or modify your communication preferences, visit us at www.ReaderService.com/consumerschoice.

SDES10R

FOR EVERY MOOD™

Spotlight on

Classic

Quintessential, modern love stories that are romance at its finest.

See the next page to enjoy a sneak peek from the Harlequin® Romance series.

CATCLASSHR10

See below for a sneak peek from our classic Harlequin® Romance® line.

Introducing DADDY BY CHRISTMAS by Patricia Thayer.

MIA caught sight of Jarrett when he walked into the open lobby. It was hard not to notice the man. In a charcoal business suit with a crisp white shirt and striped tie covered by a dark trench coat, he looked more Wall Street than small-town Colorado.

Mia couldn't blame him for keeping his distance. He was probably tired of taking care of her.

Besides, why would a man like Jarrett McKane be interested in her? Why would he want to take on a woman expecting a baby? Yet he'd done so many things for her. He'd been there when she'd needed him most. How could she not care about a man like that?

Heart pounding in her ears, she walked up behind him. Jarrett turned to face her. "Did you get enough sleep last night?"

"Yes, thanks to you," she said, wondering if he'd thought about their kiss. Her gaze went to his mouth, then she quickly glanced away. "And thank you for not bringing up my meltdown."

Jarrett couldn't stop looking at Mia. Blue was definitely her color, bringing out the richness of her eyes.

"What meltdown?" he said, trying hard to focus on what she was saying. "You were just exhausted from lack of sleep and worried about your baby."

He couldn't help remembering how, during the night, he'd kept going in to watch her sleep. How strange was that? "I hope you got enough rest."

She nodded. "Plenty. And you're a good neighbor for

HREXP1210

coming to my rescue."

He tensed. Neighbor? *What neighbor kisses you like I did?* "That's me, just the full-service landlord," he said, trying to keep the sarcasm out of his voice. He started to leave, but she put her hand on his arm.

"Jarrett, what I meant was you went beyond helping me." Her eyes searched his face. "I've asked far too much of you."

"Did you hear me complain?"

She shook her head. "You should. I feel like I've taken advantage."

"Like I said, I haven't minded."

"And I'm grateful for everything..."

Grasping her hand on his arm, Jarrett leaned forward. The memory of last night's kiss had him aching for another. "I didn't do it for your gratitude, Mia."

Gorgeous tycoon Jarrett McKane has never believed in Christmas—but he can't help being drawn to soon-to-be-mom Mia Saunders! Christmases past were spent alone...and now Jarrett may just have a fairy-tale ending for all his Christmases future!

Available December 2010, only from Harlequin® Romance®.

HREXP1210

USA TODAY **bestselling authors**

MAUREEN CHILD

and

SANDRA HYATT

UNDER THE MILLIONAIRE'S MISTLETOE

Just when these leading men thought they had it all figured out, they quickly learn their hearts have made other plans. Two passionate stories about love, longing and the infinite possibilities of kissing under the mistletoe.

Available December wherever you buy books.

Always Powerful, Passionate and Provocative.

Visit Silhouette Books at www.eHarlequin.com

SD73069

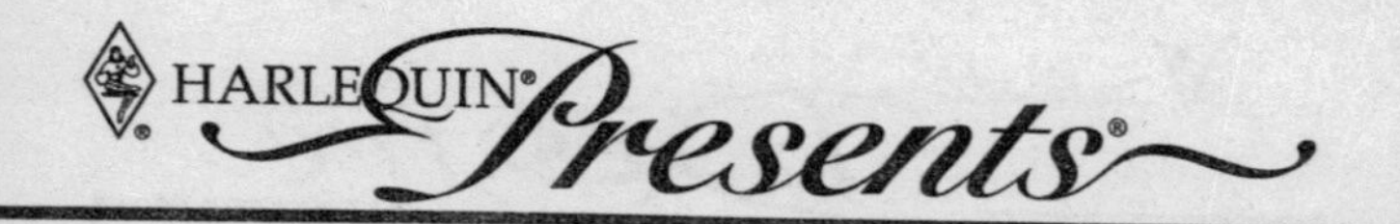

Bestselling Harlequin Presents® author

Julia James

brings you her most powerful book yet...

FORBIDDEN OR FOR BEDDING?

The shamed mistress...

Guy de Rochemont's name is a byword for wealth and power—and now his duty is to wed.

Alexa Harcourt knows she can never be anything more than *The de Rochemont Mistress.*

But Alexa—the one woman Guy wants—is also the one woman whose reputation forbids him to take her as his wife....

Available from Harlequin Presents December 2010

www.eHarlequin.com

HP12960